HARD TEXAS WINTER

HARD TEXAS WINTER

PRESTON LEWIS

WHEELER PUBLISHING
A part of Gale, a Cengage Company

Farmington Hills, Mich • San Francisco • New York • Waterville, Maine
Meriden, Conn • Mason, Ohio • Chicago

Copyright © 1981, 2018 by Preston Lewis.
Wheeler Publishing, a part of Gale, a Cengage Company.

LIBRARY OF CONGRESS CIP DATA ON FILE.
CATALOGUING IN PUBLICATION FOR THIS BOOK
IS AVAILABLE FROM THE LIBRARY OF CONGRESS

ISBN-13: 978-1-4328-5167-5 (softcover)

Published in 2018 by arrangement with Preston Lewis

Printed in the United States of America
1 2 3 4 5 6 7 22 21 20 19 18

For Mother,
the first book of her first son.

CHAPTER 1

Listless eyes strained down the dusty road for the town of Crossrock, the next destination of the tired man sheathed in a long, gray greatcoat. Morgan Garrett had hoped to get farther across Texas before the cold weather settled in, but he was just as weary as his plodding chestnut mount. Texas was just as big as everyone had said. The cold north wind from a gray sky argued against Garrett traveling much farther. The wind's chilling breath told him he would not reach his goal of Sante Fe or beyond this year; not until spring would that be possible.

As the wind howled, it seemed to be the very soul of the land. A particularly strong gust blew past Garrett, leaving his left sleeve swinging like the pendulum in a grandfather clock. The withered left limb made it difficult for Garrett to wipe from his eyes the dust stirred up by the temperamental wind, but he managed awkwardly with his rein-filled right hand.

Since he had crossed the Sabine River and ridden into Texas a few weeks back, Garrett had not seen the blackened shells of buildings, the damaged bridges and roads and the mangled landscape that he had crossed between Alabama and the Texas border. Still, the Texas land showed the effects of war, a war which didn't leave enough young men at home to plant and work the fields, to build and repair the towns, to herd and market the cattle. In those fields which four years ago would have had fine stands of cotton already being picked, grew weeds or pitiful crops unworthy of the name. This was the time of year when the cotton crops should have looked their most productive. Picking would have been well under way by now with the fields animated by families of workers pulling their long sacks down each row. Instead Garrett saw no life in the fields or in the occasional cabins he passed. Where there weren't fields stood stands of post and live oaks. The bluestem grass fought against the wind, looking as if it were waving at westbound travelers. Mesquite and juniper bushes mingled with the other vegetation and slowly Garrett realized this untamed acreage was increasing at the expense of the once-cultivated fields. Garrett was reaching the settled edge of West Texas.

His steed plodded forward down the road as weary of the journey as Garrett; but, like other cavalry horses, it was accustomed to long, tiresome marches. This trip had not been at near the pace of some past rides, and the chestnut had long since made peace with the light cavalry saddle marked "C.S.A." and with the firm-handed rider.

Both horse and rider made a gaunt picture, their bodies thin and worn. With a little more weight and rest, both would have been handsome. The horse was dignified and carried its brown head high, but with such a bony frame that pride was easily misinterpreted for wide-eyed fright. When prodded by the rider, the chestnut would seem to dance in a lively gait, but both the horse and rider cared little for such displays. With several weeks of rest and a bountiful supply of hay and oats, the chestnut could regain some of its former vigor and would still make a horse its owner could be proud of. Garrett realized, however, that the steed would never have the endurance and speed it once had.

Except for the withered arm, Garrett, with a month of good meals behind him, would have been a striking figure, too. Like the horse, he would never possess the strength of his youth for, although still young, he had aged fast during four years of war. His sandy brown hair, long and unkempt, stuck in patches from beneath his broad-rimmed, gray hat and bristled in the wind. His face was gaunt with high cheekbones that exaggerated his leanness. His bronzed skin accentuated steel-gray eyes, his most striking feature. His six-foot frame sat well in the saddle.

Ahead Garrett spied a solitary rider approaching him on the road. Here was a massive man, who almost seemed to dwarf his coal black mount. Garrett could see the rider holding a double-barreled shotgun. When the two men drew closer to one another, their mounts picked up the pace, as if trying to impress each other. Garrett could see the ruddy-faced man clearly now and was amazed at his huge shoulders and powerful arms. No doubt this man did hard work. The eyes of the two met as their horses came within talking distance. Garrett spoke first.

"How much farther to Crossrock?"

"Just 'bout two miles the way you're headed, Johnny," the red-headed rider responded in reference to the revealing gray coat Garrett was wearing.

"Is there a place to eat? I could use a good

meal," Garrett said, ignoring the note of contempt in the rider's voice.

"I don't know as if I would say it is good, but you can get a meal at the Benton Saloon. If you've got no more questions, I'd like to get on with my hunting."

"Nothing more than thanks. What be your game?"

"After turkey today. It wasn't too many months back, though, I was after gray coats like yourself."

"I didn't expect to run into too many Yanks, particularly one with something in his craw, here in Texas. Now don't tell me Texas wasn't a Confederate state just a few months back 'cause I know better."

"You're right, Johnny, but you're in Madden County and we voted against secession, though not all of us. Now if you have been traveling this road all day then you've passed through Flores and Meachum counties and they didn't vote to go with the Confederacy either."

"Mister, I'm not riding west to refight a war that's finished. I mean no trouble. Thank you for your time and good day."

With that Garrett turned his own eyes from his adversary's. Garrett's legs tightened just a bit in his saddle, making the almost imperceptible signal that told the chestnut it was time to resume the journey.

The other man, too, went his separate way, not having noticed Garrett's lame arm. Just the gray greatcoat with the faded gold braid in a double knot that signified a captain's rank had been enough to command his attention. Bill Murphy resented that uniform and what it stood for. Indiana born, Murphy had moved to Texas as a kid eleven years ago. When war broke out, Murphy, like many of his Madden County neighbors who had migrated from the north, returned to his previous home and joined the Union Army. It was a cause Murphy had believed in rabidly, but that fervor had turned to bitterness after his lifelong friend Tom had been killed in a battle with the gray coats.

The cold wind blew with vengeance that chilled both Garrett and Murphy. Knowing he was drawing closer to Crossrock increased Garrett's appetite for a hot meal. For Murphy the wind took the fun out of his turkey shooting. About the same time Murphy approached his favorite hunting spot, Garrett rode over a small rise in the increasingly flat landscape and could make out the town of Crossrock. Relief from hunger was finally in sight.

From the distance he could see about a

dozen buildings on the main road through town. Behind those buildings were an assortment of houses, which before the war some 150 people of Crossrock called their homes. Now probably no more than half that number remained. Beyond the town Garrett could discern the streambed of the North Fork of the Brazos. At the far edge of the slow-moving waters, Garrett could make out a huge stone, roughly shaped like a cross and the namesake of the town. Beyond the river, which was a misnomer by the standards of his Alabama home, the landscape grew rougher and more desolate.

Drawing closer to Crossrock, Garrett could tell that several of the false-fronted buildings on the main street were boarded up. One of those that was not in use had a faded sign that read "Boarding House." That worried Garrett for he was going to need a place to stay. Although he had no more than three dollars in his pocket, he hoped that would get him by until he could find work that would pay enough over the coming winter months to rent shelter. Garrett, who a year ago did not have to worry about having only one good arm, was disturbed by the prospect of not finding work. It was hard for a one-armed man to chop wood or make shelter along the trail.

Perhaps in a few years, after he had adjusted to his infirmity, Garrett's lame arm would pose no threat to survival. But today's cold winds worried him, although his battle worn countenance did not betray that concern.

Crossrock was not a colorful town. The buildings were mostly of unpainted wood and they seemed almost to meld into the countryside. Were it not for the plumes of smoke that rose from a few of the chimneys, a rider passing more than a mile away from the town might not have even noticed its existence. Besides the abandoned buildings, which were the most colorless of all, Garrett rode past a combined livery stable and blacksmith shop, two general stores and the Benton Saloon, which had received the qualified recommendation from the broad-shouldered man Garrett had encountered on the road.

Between the saloon and the North Fork of the Brazos were a few more buildings, including a boot and saddle shop, a billiard hall and a vacant bank. Normally, Garrett would have taken care of his chestnut mount first, but his hungry stomach growled like the wind and he wanted to inquire about room and job possibilities. If prospects looked good, he would take the horse to the livery stable and use whatever it took of his remaining money to get the chestnut combed down and fed. If Garrett was unsuccessful, he guessed he would keep moving west and hope for the best. Before going inside, he allowed his mount to quench its thirst at a trough of cold water and tied it to a hitching post in front of the saloon.

Opening one of the weathered double doors that kept the brisk wind outside, Garrett was met by a pleasant warmth which immediately soothed his aching body. What he saw before him was not a large saloon. A half-dozen tables were scattered about the cozy confines with three on each side of the path through the sawdust that led to the dark wood bar. Only the table in the far corner of the room was occupied and five men sat there near the potbellied stove, absorbing the heat. Behind the bar a squat man with a heavy black mustache was carrying plates from the counter into a back room. Picking up another load, he eyed Garrett slowly.

"How about a drink, mister?"

"I'd prefer some food and I was told yours was about the best there was in town."

"It's all there is in town that's for sale. Anyway, I was just taking what was left back into the kitchen, but you're welcome to what's here. Probably cold by now. It doesn't stay warm long on a day like this, but it still should be enough to keep your belly from bellowing."

"Never really heard it put that way, but I guess you're right," Garrett said, reaching into his pocket. "How much is it?"

"When there's plenty of it and it's warm, it's 20 cents, but I'll let you have what you can get for 15 cents. Fair enough?"

"Fair enough."

"Maude, bring that plate of meat and the bread back out here. We've got one more to feed."

As Garrett moved to the far end of the bar where two plates of food were waiting, he came face to face with Maude Benton. Like her husband, she was short and squat. No doubt that she had eaten more than her share of the leftovers from the daily lunch counter.

"Howdy," she said, as she looked Garrett over. And before he could begin to help his plate, she noticed the limp left sleeve of his coat.

"Want me to fill your plate for you?" she inquired. "You just tell me what you want and how much of it and leave the rest to me."

"Much obliged," Garrett acquiesced. He

watched as she filled his plate to her own satisfaction.

"Where you from?"

"Now, Maude," her husband interrupted, "the man's hungry and he don't want your talking to interfere with his eating."

"You just don't worry none about that," she scolded her husband, "sometimes an appetite for conversation can be just as big as a hunger for food. Now you go see if you can find me a couple more slices of bread."

Garrett chuckled as the barkeeper left the counter.

"Alabama was my home, but no more."

"Lot like you these days, bound to be, because that war done changed everything up. Can't lose a whole generation of men and things not be different. Nothing's been the same here since it all started and I doubt if people's suspicions about one another are ever going to die down around these parts. Where's that bread, Wallace?"

"Here it is, just keep patient," the barkeeper said on his return. "Now don't pay her no mind. She just talks too much and always gets herself in trouble because of it."

"No bother," said Garrett, "riding solitar' does tend to make you want a little conversation now and then, although it will never replace eating."

Maude Benton carried the plate over to the table on the other side of the stove from the five men Garrett had observed when he entered.

"Now you sit down here where the stove can keep you warm," Maude said. "This food ought to help perk you up, too."

"If it don't kill him first," interrupted one of the quintet at the nearby table to the laughter of his companions.

Maude Benton sneered with contempt at the table as Garrett took off his coat.

"You just take a seat and ignore those boys. They're troublemakers. I'll go get you some sweet potato coffee."

"Sweet potato coffee?"

"Mister, you forget that there's a war that ain't been over but six months or less. For the last two years or so we hadn't had any real coffee. This is the best we can do. They may have some over at Dobbs's store, but if they got any, they ain't had it long and it costs more than you can afford."

"Then bring me a full cup and I'll drink it no matter what," Garrett said, as he laid his coat over a chair by the stove. Taking another chair, this one facing the wall, he sat down to consume his meal.

The whispering from the table with the five men, or troublemakers as Maude Benton called them, caught Garrett's attention and he knew they were talking about him. But the crackling and popping of the wood in the stove prevented him from hearing what was said. With his limp arm resting on the table, he attacked the plate of vittles. The dark meat had a rather sweet taste to it, and he was uncertain what it was. Deciding that since the coffee came from sweet potatoes, it might not be best to inquire about the meat, Garrett ate in silence. When Maude returned with the cup of coffee, he took a couple swallows, relishing it more for its warmth than its flavor.

Halfway through his meal, he tried to ignore the five men at the other table as they got up to leave. But one of the five strode past Garrett's table and knocked his greatcoat from the chair onto the sawdust-covered floor.

"Oh, I'm sorry, soldier boy," he said in mock sorrow, "but just a little bump and that coat fell just like the whole Confederate army."

The man's companions laughed uproariously, and Garrett looked at his detractor for the first time. He was a man of medium height and build. Some would have considered the man's boyish face handsome. His brown eyes seemed almost to sparkle and his mouth was turned up in a sly grin. His rounded face and small nose seemed almost too perfect. And perhaps they would have been were it not for two parallel scars that ran down his right cheek almost from his ear to his lip. A brown mustache attempted to hide the twin scars, but it served only to accentuate them and further mar his otherwise handsome appearance.

After a hard look at the man, Garrett bent over to retrieve his coat.

"Here, let me do that," the man insisted. "After all, I bet it's hard for a one-hander to brush the sawdust off."

More laughter from the man's cohorts was met by continued silence from Garrett. The Bentons, who had stopped cleaning up the luncheon counter, stared mutely.

"Say, mister, one more thing. You want me to cut up your meat for you?"

To a chorus of redoubled laughter the five men walked out the door. The last one through failed to shut it so the next gust of wind blew it open with an impact that rattled the windows. Wallace Benton, cursing, ran to shut the flapping door and Maude strode over to Garrett's table.

"Some clientele you've got here," Garrett said before Maude could open her mouth.

"They're troublemakers, I told you," she

growled. "Half the problems Crossrock had during the war can be attributed to those boys. You can't prove it, but they were the ones that made Madden County unsafe during the war. The decent men in this county enlisted in the army, either Union or Confederate, and left. Brad Decker — he's the one that was baiting you — he and his boys just took advantage of a county full of women, children and old men."

"There you go again talking this fellow's head off," Wallace Benton interrupted. "Those men are just polecats and that's all that needs to be said."

"The type's common everywhere during a war," said Garrett after a minute's silence. "Back in Alabama there were some the same way."

"Bet none's as bad as Brad Decker," said Maude. "I get mad just thinking 'bout him. Guess I ought to talk about something else. Say, where you headed for, mister?"

"Now that may not be none of your concern," suggested Wallace Benton to his wife.

"It's no great secret, Mr. Benton, because I'm unsure of my destination," said Garrett. "I had thought about getting to Santa Fe or maybe even going onto California, but that was when I thought I would make better

21

time. With the weather getting colder, I guess I am going to have to stop somewhere, if I can find some work."

"These are hard times, mister, and jobs don't exist in many places and Crossrock is like the rest," said the barkeeper, who took a seat at Garrett's table. "Sure, there's some work to be done, plenty of it, but nobody's got any money to pay for seeing it done."

"What about on down the road?"

"Mister, there ain't much between here and wherever you're headed. The road begins to peter out from Crossrock west until there's little more than a trail."

"Anyway," said Maude, "with no soldiers to patrol west of here the last four years, the Comanches and Kiowas have made the country unsafe for man and beast. You'd better think about staying here, if you can, unless you want to face some Indians single-handedly."

The woman had barely gotten the sentence out of her mouth before she realized it had been a poor choice of words.

"I'm sorry, mister, I didn't mean that the way it sounded."

"What'd I tell you, Maude, you've always used too much mouth and too little brain," Benton scolded.

"It's just one of those things," Garrett

22

replied. "No harm done."

"Just the same, I didn't want to sound like that mangy Brad Decker," said Maude.

Garrett returned to his meal and the Bentons resumed their chores around the saloon. Wallace Benton brought in some more firewood, putting another log in the stove and filling the woodbox. Maude wiped down the tables. Garrett was silently angered by the insults of Brad Decker. It was, he imagined, the type of vindictive remarks he would have to get accustomed to for the remainder of his life. If he only had two good hands, he would have responded to Decker's insults, Garrett thought, but then he realized it was useless to think in terms of something that would never again be. The sooner he got used to the cutting remarks and adjusted to his one-armed existence, the better his chances would be for carving out a productive life for himself.

Interrupting his thoughts, Maude Benton asked if he would like some pie. After learning it was sweet potato pie, Garrett turned down the offer. The sweet potato coffee had about filled his appetite for that ugly orange vegetable which Garrett had always despised. After the filling, if not entirely delicious, meal Garrett sat pondering his future. If prospects were bad in Crossrock, they sounded even worse on the road to Santa Fe for the Bentons had confirmed what he had heard about the Indians at previous stops.

The saloon's solitary patron found his situation ironic at best. It had not been too many months past that his future had seemed well plotted and secure. It was not a large plantation by Southern standards, but it was big enough and it made Garrett the largest landowner in Mallory County, Alabama. Garrett had been expected to take up where his father, one of the original settlers in Mallory County, had stopped when he died nine months before Fort Sumter. And young Garrett had disappointed none of his neighbors. Despite his youth, his savvy and his good management ability caught the eyes of many who had even talked about him running for state legislature. It was no surprise either that when war broke out, Garrett organized a company of cavalry and was immediately elected to head the outfit.

The war had been a long one for him because he had seen too many of his neighbors die beside him. When it was over Garrett returned to his land, or what had once been his land. But Union vultures moved in almost as quickly as the surrender was signed and took over the title by questionable means. Once he got home, Garrett found out that the land, except for a small plot, did not mean that much to him any more. On that little rectangle of ground was buried his mother and father, both of whom had died before the war. Beside those two graves, however, were three newer mounds of dirt, the final resting place of Garrett's wife and two young sons. It was easier to move on than to rebuild his life around those memories of Mallory County. After leaving some wild flowers on each of the three graves, Garrett began the ride west, not even stopping to tell his intentions to his neighbors who were still living.

Perhaps the new country out west was too much of a challenge for a one-armed man. No doubt the hardships would be greater, but the Southern states were going to endure the pain of rebuilding, and the prospects for a just reconstruction had probably died with Lincoln. Had he stopped anywhere between Mallory County and Texas, the similarities with his old way of life would have been too great for comfort. Texas, meanwhile, was more primitive, more arid, more open. Garrett wanted a complete change and the near desolate country around Crossrock did provide that. The longer Garrett thought, the more convinced he became that staying in Crossrock was the right decision for now. But since that decision was contingent on at least finding shelter, he knew that even it might not be final.

Looking up from the table and turning toward the bar, Garrett broke the silence. "I've thought it over and the two of you make it seem like I have no choice but to stay the winter here in Crossrock."

"Aw, don't let Maude scare you," Wallace Benton said. "You could probably make it to Santa Fe before the really bad weather sets in and without getting scalped, but there's few other places between here and there where you can have a roof over your head."

"Do you have a notion where I could stay?"

"Well, that's a good question. I don't know that I do. Ever since the boarding house was closed there hasn't been much available. Of course, there hasn't been much need for a boarding house around here lately, either."

"What about a job then?"

"Another good question that I don't have a good answer for. Like I told you earlier, there's not much money left to pay help with. Those that's got a little money, though, are likely to be those that cast their lot with the North. You have any ideas, Maude?"

"Are you sure you want me to talk?" she said to her husband. "I've been thinking, but I don't come up with much. Bill Murphy might could use some help, but since he is cutting wood and clearing land, I doubt you'd be what he was looking for. Even if you were, he probably wouldn't hire you. He's a bit contrary."

"Anybody else?" asked her husband.

"Well, what about old man Dobbs? I understand he has been thinking about somebody to help out with the store. Goodness knows he could use it. That girl just don't pull much weight when it comes to pitching in."

"What do you mean?" asked Garrett, who had already decided at least to inquire at the general store he had ridden past on the way in.

Wallace Benton just stood quietly for a moment, ignoring Garrett's question until Garrett asked again.

"Let me just put it this way, I don't think you're exactly what the man is looking for."

"It's the arm. Isn't it?" Garrett asked as he stood and put on his greatcoat.

"No, that's not it at all. You see, like I told

you before, this war created some dislikes among the people in this county. It's your coat, mister, that worries me. It's gray. Dobbs's only boy wore blue and he never returned from the war."

CHAPTER 2

Outside the wind hummed a threatening song. The biting dust and cold temperatures discouraged unnecessary ventures out of doors. When Morgan Garrett left the saloon, he found himself on a street devoid of life. His chestnut, a couple of horses down the street toward the stream crossing, and a wagon team at the other end of town were the only living things in sight. The solitude bothered Garrett. Except for the whispering wind, it was like the unnatural quiet that often preceded a cavalry engagement. On those occasions, that abnormal tranquility of the elements quickly vanished in a thunder of exploding powder and human anguish. How far away that uneasy feeling seemed; and yet, how closely it hugged the empty street in Crossrock, Texas. Garrett could only guess that it was a case of battle nerves, clouding his perceptions. He had survived, but war had attuned his senses to an unnaturally cautious and suspicious degree.

Wrapping his greatcoat tighter around himself, Garrett turned to his mount. The chestnut acted uncomfortable in the brisk wind and the blowing dirt. Although his slim financial resources were now the cost of a meal less than when he had arrived in town, Garrett was determined to feed and bed the horse properly. He led the horse back down the street toward the livery stable he had passed on the way in.

Garrett passed Dobbs General Store as he headed up the street, walking his horse toward a meal and rest. Slowing his pace, he looked in at the store, but he saw no one. Moving on, he found himself facing a drafty building in need of repair. This was the livery stable. Opening the double doors that were large enough to admit a wagon, Garrett walked in with the horse. It was a darkened cavern, lighted only by a few rays that seeped in through the holes in the roof, and it smelled of horse dung and dry hay. It wasn't much, but it would at least offer the chestnut some protection from the frigid winds after sundown.

"Be with you in a minute," yelled a husky voice from behind one of the far stalls.

Garrett waited, observing the stable's tenants which included several horses, a lazy dog, a buggy, and a buckboard wagon. In a far corner was a surprisingly big stack of hay.

"What do you need?" said the same voice that had greeted Garrett a few minutes earlier.

Stepping out from behind the stall this side of the hay, a muscular but wrinkled man strode into Garrett's view. The strong arms and the battered hands bore the scars of hearth and anvil.

"I want to put my horse up for the night. Can you accommodate me?"

"Sure, mister, you got the money?"

"It depends."

"On what?"

"What you charge?"

"It's 25 cents the first night for hay and combing him down and 20 cents a day after that. Payment in advance."

"I've got the money," said Garrett digging into his pocket for his next-to-last dollar. "Here's for two nights and for some extra fodder for him."

"You got a deal."

Garrett handed over the reins and followed the man back to a rear stall. The liveryman took off the saddlebags and bedroll and handed them to Garrett. As he did, the liveryman noticed Garrett's lame left arm beneath the faded Confederate-issue coat. The man began to uncinch the saddle.

"We don't see many saddles like this around these parts. What is it, cavalry?"

"That's what it was. I rode it enough months to get used to it and it is lighter than most saddles."

"Yeah, I notice by your left arm there you probably need a light one. How did it happen?"

"Got shot. Can't say much more. Just got shot like a lot of others."

The conversation stopped for a few minutes as the liveryman finished unsaddling the chestnut and went to get some feed for the tired animal. After he returned with fodder, the liveryman took a curry comb and began to work on the animal.

"You've got a pretty light touch for a blacksmith."

"Ain't the touch," snorted the gray-haired liveryman. "It's age. Getting old has improved my stable work, but hurt my blacksmithing. Just can't keep the pace like I once could. Besides, horses make better company than hammers and anvils."

"We've all got our problems," Garrett said to himself as much as to the aging black-

32

smith. "I guess I will leave him in your hands. Take good care of him while I try to find a place to stay the night."

"Don't expect too much luck. The boarding house is closed. If you can't find something, come on back and you can sleep here for the night. A veteran like yourself ought not to find these accommodations too bad. At least you can find some hay to sleep on instead of the bare ground and there are some horse blankets scattered about to keep you warm."

"Much obliged to you, mister. I may have to take you up on that tonight."

"Don't call me 'mister.' The name's Holcomb, John Henry Holcomb."

"Okay, Holcomb it is. I may see you later."

Slinging his saddlebags and bedroll over his shoulder, Garrett left the liveryman at work on his horse and returned to the cold, dusty street. The shadows were growing longer as Garrett marched toward the Dobbs General Store. Sundown was no more than two hours away and time was running out on this miserable day and on Garrett's job prospects. The strong winds played tag with several tumbleweeds which raced ahead of Garrett. He stepped on the plank sidewalk and strode past the general store, peering inside like an army scout spying on the enemy. He was surprised at the shelves which were better stocked than he had expected after his talk with the Bentons. Maybe the full shelves improved his chances for work. Behind the rear counter, Garrett spied an aproned figure waiting on a customer. That must be Dobbs. But there was another figure he noticed, too — a young woman seated behind the counter near the front window. She was intently reading a book and didn't look up as Garrett walked by.

Although his glimpse of her had been only brief, Garrett was struck by the gentle quality of her looks. Long brown hair framed a pale face. She sat perfectly erect and her upright posture pulled the pale yellow blouse with the buttonup collar taut. Her face was a soft contrast to the hardy Texas surroundings which made even more stunning her beauty. Her erectness and the precise way she held her head while reading bespoke well of her social training. Such refinement seemed alien this far west in Texas.

Drawing a deep breath, Garrett opened the door, which jingled from a bell hung on the inside knob, and walked into the warmth of the store. It was no surprise that the aproned man behind the back counter did not acknowledge his presence, but kept filling the order of an old, wrinkled woman who looked too frail to be out on the streets on such a windy day. It did surprise Garrett, however, that the young woman at the side counter continued reading her book, ignoring him even after he had closed the door to the wind which had invited itself into the room.

Garrett advanced to the side counter where the young woman was seated. With each step he became even more astounded at the woman's gentle good looks. Her face bespoke the innocence of a young girl while her frame was that of a mature woman. Only after he had reached the counter and placed his saddlebags and bedroll on it did she look up.

"Can I help you?"

"No, I believe I need to talk to your father."

"How did you know he was my father?" she asked. "You've never been in here before."

"Hired help," said Garrett, "wouldn't persist in reading a book once a customer walked in the door so you had to be a relative. I figured you for a daughter, not a wife."

The comment ignited a fire in her blue

eyes that showed not a childlike, but a womanly determination not to be ridiculed. There was something else in the eyes, too, perhaps an ounce of deceit that detracted from her otherwise flawless beauty.

Pausing long enough to shut her book with a convincing clap, she stood up and replied, "If a customer doesn't look like he's going to buy anything, I see no hurry unless in hastening his departure."

Garrett smiled at her and took in the soft features of her face. "You win," he said. "Until now I didn't realize the meager contents of my pockets were so visible."

"Not many boys wearing gray uniforms have much spending money these days," she said. "Sure, they may be rich with Confederate dollars, but we just take United States currency here. Father will be through in a moment and you can talk to him. Unless you desire to make a purchase, then I shall continue with my reading, undisturbed, I hope, by the shadow of your presence."

The woman's spunkiness impressed Garrett, who picked up his belongings from the counter and began to walk around the tables in the center of the store and to examine the walls of supplies. For the first time, the mingled odors of the room intrigued him as he tried to untangle them. Yes, there was coffee in Dobbs General Store because Garrett caught the fleeting aroma among the many that united into an amalgamation of sharp, but not unpleasant smells. All the aromas, though, were tinged with the fragrance of burning mesquite wood in the stove at the center of the store. Garrett gravitated toward that stove because of its comfortable warmth. He waited nervously, pacing around the stove until the wrinkled woman picked up her basket of groceries and left, the tinkling of the bell on the door signalling her departure.

Garrett looked up at the aproned man who was walking around the counter and toward him. It was the first time he had really examined the man he hoped would hire him. Dobbs's features were sharp and his blue eyes piercing, like those of his daughter, and his nose straight and narrow. His mouth was fixed in a perpetual frown which made his mood hard to read. There was some resemblance, if one looked hard enough, between father and daughter. The man's brown hair was the same shade as his daughter's except that his was now muted with strands of gray. Once again, Garrett realized he was nervous, as he had been before he had entered the door.

"Mr. Dobbs," he said, extending his good

right hand, "I am Morgan Garrett from Mallory County, Alabama, on route to points west. Cold weather, though, is not a good traveling companion and I seek to stay in Crossrock until spring, if I can find work. I've heard you might be in a way of needing some help. That true?"

The storekeeper just stood there taking in Garrett from head to foot. At first, Garrett thought he should not have worn the gray uniform coat to meet Dobbs. But the longer Dobbs stood there, the less certain Garrett became of that. Eventually, Dobbs would find out one way or another because it is hard to hide four years of your past. And what else could he have worn? All his clothes were army-issue gray. Dobbs's frown gave Garrett an unfavorable reading on the man's response, but the Alabaman could see that the daughter had stopped her reading and was staring intently at her father.

"You rode into town today, did you not?" Dobbs finally broke the silence and then answered his own question with a nod. "What you saw mostly was fields, empty fields, and where you saw any crops at all, they were poor crops. There's going to be very little money made in these parts this year. Little money for the farmer means very little for the merchant. And that means little business and little need for help."

The young woman smugly returned to her reading once her father had finished speaking. Garrett, however, tried to regather his thoughts and respond to Dobbs, but before he spoke, Dobbs continued.

"Of course, if a man didn't ask for much and was willing to do some work, he might be able to convince me that he was worth hiring."

Immediately, the man's daughter stopped her reading, shut her book loudly and walked over to join the two men.

"Money is of little use to a man who cannot buy shelter and that is what worries me most," Garrett said. "If you could house me and give me enough for food for my horse, that's all I should ask."

The young woman, her eyes flaming once again, was glaring at her father, feeling betrayed by his readiness to hire the same man who had only moments before been rude to her. Her face was flushed with anger.

"Father, can we really afford this?"

"Just go about your reading, Peg, I'll handle this."

Turning to Garrett, the old man continued, "Can you keep a ledger book?"

"Yes," said Garrett, "I've done it for a

cotton operation and I'm sure with a little help I could catch on quickly to your store books."

"What about your arm? Can you lift a sack of flour or load a wagon with supplies?"

"Not as well as I once could nor as quickly, but one good working arm I do have. One good arm is better than two lazy ones and I'll make you a good man, if you'll give me a chance."

"Your hands don't worry me as much as your politics," said Dobbs, his forehead furrowed. "I lost my boy in the war and you should know that my beliefs and yours are different. There'll be no discussion of politics by you with me or my customers. What customers I have believe like I do. Those that don't generally trade at the other store down the street. Is that understood?"

Garrett nodded, saying nothing. Peg Dobbs, however, wasn't speechless.

"Father, we don't need to do this. We can handle things fine as we've done since Mother died. That's been almost a year now. Won't you at least think about this? If you need a strong man to help you, then Billy can give you two good arms when you need them. I can handle the ledger, too, and you know that."

"Peg, I have my reasons for hiring him and they are of greater concern to me than your reasons for sending him away. I don't want to hear any more from you on it. The decision has been made."

Dobbs, extending his right hand, turned back to Garrett and hired him with a handshake.

"There's too little time left today to get you started so we'll begin most of that tomorrow. There are a few things, though, you must know. We open at eight o'clock so I expect to see you up an hour before then and ready to begin when I get here at seven."

Garrett listened to Dobbs's instructions about opening the store, keeping the extra key and maintaining fire in the stove. At five o'clock Dobbs sent Peggy home. The young woman had stayed out of the way since her father hired Garrett. She fumed over the decision and had not once spoken to the stranger that only an hour ago had entered the store so rudely. Once Peggy left for home, Dobbs made sure Garrett had taken care of his horse.

"My daughter and I live a couple hundred feet from here," Dobbs told Garrett, "and I just don't feel that's close enough to keep a proper watch on the store anymore. That's

41

one reason I hired you. During the war when nobody had anything to begin with, it wasn't a problem, but now that I've been able to rebuild my stock a little, I'm afraid some people are going to want some of my merchandise without paying for it."

Dobbs led his new employee behind the back counter, through a door and into a small supply room and office. Against the wall that separated the room from the front was a cot, covered with quilts.

"That's going to be your bed," Dobbs said. "It may not be the most comfortable in Texas, but it sure beats that hard, cold ground."

"It looks fine to me. It's probably more than I will ever be able to repay you for."

"If you keep a watch over my store and people know that you're here, then I will be compensated," Dobbs responded. "I noticed when you took off your coat you wore no sidearm. Do you have a gun?"

"In my saddlebags I've got a revolver, but I'm low on shells."

"My shells are under the back counter, help yourself. I hope you don't need them, but they're there just the same."

"I hope not, too, I've had enough of shooting at other men to last me."

"That's what you would think would be

the case for most men in these parts, but it ain't so. The war may have settled the question on secession and slavery, but here in Madden County it created unneighborly feelings."

"Yeah, that's what I gather from a little conversation I had with a big fellow on the road into town."

"Madden County was split pretty even on the secession question and it wouldn't be so bad now were there only Unionists and Confederates. But we've got some bushwhackers, more the outlaw element than anything else, who are agitating these bad feelings. Most of these are boys that stayed here during the war and plagued women and children and robbed old men. It's just inevitable that there is going to be trouble."

"Maybe things won't be so bad," offered Garrett.

"It would be nice, but I know the leader of the bushwhackers. He's lazy and no good. A troublemaker named Decker, Brad Decker."

"Afraid I have met your man."

"How? You haven't been in town long have you?"

"I got here about an hour past high sun and took a lunch at the Benton Saloon. Decker was there and had a little fun with my bad arm."

"That's him all right. He runs around most of the time with four others, all just as mean, but none as smart. He's cagey as a cougar."

"I'll keep an eye out for him."

"You'd best do that because he always brings trouble."

The conversation stopped with the jingling of the bell on the door. Out of the wind came a man and woman wanting to purchase flour, dry beans and some kerosene. As Dobbs went to assist the couple, he told Garrett to rearrange the back room as best he could to meet his needs.

In the shadowy room that would be his home for the next few months, Garrett stood surveying the contents. No doubt it would be cramped for there were crates, barrels and bundles scattered throughout, but it would also be warm, a situation that was most pleasing to the former soldier. Saving the best three for bedding, Garrett unstacked the quilts from the worn cot and restacked them on some wooden crates nearby. With a dozen quilts stacked within reaching distance of his cot, Garrett grew smug about the winter.

Across the door from his cot was Dobbs's rolltop. It was a large, imposing desk with pigeonholes stuffed full of papers. Atop the desk were the bound black ledger books. Garrett opened the top one and thumbed through its pages. He found three different handwritings on the pages of varying smudged neatness. It didn't look like the record-keeping method would be too difficult to pick up.

In closing the ledger, Garrett spied by the adjacent wall a four-tiered bookshelf. It was filled with books of all shapes and sizes. On the top shelf were several readers and arithmetic books for schoolroom use. Peggy Dobbs must teach school, thought Garrett. On the remaining shelves, Garrett discovered books he never expected to find west of New Orleans. There were tomes by Shakespeare, Rousseau, Voltaire, Sophocles, Moliere, Milton, Scott and others — three shelves full of the classics. Garrett could not believe it. How long had it been since he had read any of them? He could not remember because the four years of war had muted all his prior experiences. The sight of the books took him on a journey back to the years when he had attended the academy. At first he had found the books a boring chore that the taskmaster demanded. Later that changed and Garrett grew to appreciate much of the literature he was exposed

45

to. It even came in useful when he was courting Molly, his dead wife, as Garrett had often used a remembered line or two as they sat on the porch or walked together in the woods. When Garrett had business down at Mobile, he would sometimes remember an appropriate quotation for his letters back home to Molly. It was a habit he had continued during the war, although the letters to Molly were fewer in number and in length. Those were fine times with Molly. . . .

Garrett was surprised when he turned and found Dobbs in the room staring at him for he had not heard the ringing of the bells when the two customers left.

"You've found Peg's library," said Dobbs.

"Not a bad one at all. There are probably more books on these four shelves than I had expected to see altogether in Texas."

"Oh, that's not all," said Dobbs, "she's got another bookcase full at home. They were her mother's before she died. Like her mother, Peg reads all the time. In fact, I think she has read most of them and is going back through. You ever read any of these?"

"I had occasion to read a few of them at one time, but I haven't read anything like a book in several years now."

"I tried to read some because Beatrice was always wanting me to, but mostly I just skipped over them. My eyes tire easily and I just never could get interested in the stories or the philosophy enough to finish them."

"Beatrice must have been your wife. Was she a school teacher?"

"She was for several years when we were in Indiana, and even for a few months after we moved here. She liked it some, but just taught here until they could get someone else to do it. We decided it would be best for her to help around the store."

Dobbs pulled from his pocket a battered gold watch and checked the time. It was a quarter to six and time to begin closing up.

The proprietor showed Garrett the usual order in shutting the store for the night. It was not a long process, but several things had to be done. Garrett observed and tried to remember all that Dobbs was doing, but there was just too much for it all to soak in during one session.

"Remember now, I am hiring you as much because you have a gun as I am to help out during the day. You be sure your gun is ready."

Garrett nodded and looked out the front window into the street. There, approaching the store, was the massive rider Garrett had encountered on the road into Crossrock earlier in the day. Hanging on each side of the man's horse was a large wild turkey. The successful hunter stopped in front of the store, dismounted and walked in. Dobbs, who was facing Garrett and giving final instructions before locking up, turned to see who had entered.

"Hello, Bill. Any luck?"

"Sure did. Where's Peggy? I've got her the biggest Tom she's ever seen."

"Gone home already. I sent her on since I got me some help with closing up."

Bill Murphy looked Garrett straight in the eye for the second time during the day. Although not rude, Murphy's gruff manner left no doubt he didn't care for the new help. Garrett could see the disdain in the man's eyes.

"Hello again, Johnny. I got those turkeys just like I used to get those gray coats."

"Now Bill, that's no way to be talking to my new hand."

"Hand is right," said Bill, noticing Garrett's lameness for the first time. "When you need two good strong hands, though, what you going to do?"

"Enough of that," Dobbs retorted. "You're stubborner than Peg, if that's possible. Whether you like it or not, he is going to be helping me in more ways than you think. So just come down off your Unionist high horse and shake hands with him."

Grudgingly, Murphy extended his hand and Dobbs introduced the men by name. Murphy had a powerful grip which he used to give Garrett a crushing handshake. Garrett, however, did not flinch, but kept looking Murphy in his green eyes. At length, the two former soldiers in opposing armies broke off their handshake and turned silently to Dobbs, who was looking at his gold pocket watch.

"Well, this friendly conversation you two have been running has kept me here past closing time. Come on Bill, you can walk me home to see Peg, but I am not going to help you dress those turkeys, not in this windy weather. You'll have to do that yourself and maybe Peg will feel sorry enough for you to invite you in for supper."

Turning to Garrett, Dobbs continued, "I'm locking up now. I showed you where the extra key is in case you need to let yourself out. Otherwise, I'll be in at seven tomorrow and put you to work."

Dobbs closed and locked the door, leaving with Murphy. Garrett was relieved the day was nearing an end. He was tired. The ride into Crossrock had fatigued him.

Garrett sought rest more than food.

After making a final check of the store, he went into the backroom, crawled into bed and went to sleep. It was a sound, restful sleep which created a contented snore. Only the revolver which lay on the floor beside the cot belied the tranquility of that first night in Crossrock.

CHAPTER 3

Two weeks after that first cold night in Crossrock, Garrett felt comfortable with the storekeeping routine. It had not been hard learning where everything was kept, since most of the customers requested the same staples and goods on a regular basis. There still wasn't enough money around to spend on frills and it would be that way for a while. For those who tried to farm, it would be at least next year before the land could return them any money and for those who had cattle, it would take time to reassemble their herds. Consequently, most folks just spent what money they had on the necessities — flour, salt, beans and maybe some kerosene for their lamps.

At first, Garrett thought it was going to be hard to avoid breaking his vow of political silence that Dobbs had extracted from him. Since politics was often the main topic of the old men who would gather around

Dobbs's stove on cold days and chew the political fat, Garrett could not help but be exposed to their views and biases. The first few days he was silently angry about their stubborn insistence on refighting the war and issue of slavery. Dobbs would join in the conversations, leaving no doubt in Garrett's mind, that the store owner was a fervent abolitionist. The ever-frowning Dobbs, in the midst of those tirades, would glance at Garrett, who would be working out his silent frustrations by dusting the same rough board shelf a dozen times, and change the subject. "That's past history, of course, and it's time to get on with the present," he would say as he turned to talking about the weather or the latest gossip, anything which didn't make his hand so uncomfortable.

Gradually, Garrett's attitude changed toward the old men and he listened with amusement to their talks. After all, when there was fighting to be done, these were men who for the most part had too little stamina or too feeble a body to wage war. Texas had a way of aging men well before their time. Since they had been unable to join the army and fight, the normal instinct in times of war, these men were relegated to doing their fighting on a verbal battleground with politics the most common field of combat. Garrett often had to resist the urge to join in these wordy forays and to correct an obvious tactical blunder, but he would hold himself, as if in reserve for the proper battle. The first day after Garrett was hired, the old men around the stove were shocked that Dobbs had employed a Confederate soldier, much less a former officer. Their hushed whispers told Garrett they were talking about him, but Dobbs's resolve to keep Garrett and the fact that the Alabaman held his tongue during their discussions, gradually warmed them up to him, much as he had grown tolerant of their often repetitive discourses and arguments about the war and what might have been. In fact, when the discussion moved to something besides politics, like the weather, Garrett was included as a welcomed participant.

The weather was often a major point of discussion for it changed so much and so rapidly. It was now well into the final month of the year, and in the two weeks since Garrett had been in Crossrock, not two consecutive days had been the same. There was the cold, blustery first day when the blowing dust had made ventures outside uncomfortable at best. Then came a cloud-covered day when a light rain helped settle the dust. The following day had been warm and the day after that absolutely scorching. Cooler weather came in after that. And so it went.

Unlike the ever-changing weather, one thing remained constant those first two weeks in the store. That was the attitude of Peggy Dobbs to her father's new employee. Her displeasure was manifested by a cold indifference to the Alabaman. She virtually ignored him, never letting her blue eyes meet his and talking to him only when there was no other alternative. Seated in the cane-bottom chair behind the side counter near the window, she would spend each day reading her books and occasionally glancing out into the street. When she thought no one was looking, she would lean back, raising the chair's front legs off the floor, and rock gently. Since it was unladylike, she tried not to let anybody catch her swaying with the chair.

Despite her coldness toward him, Garrett was warmed every day by the sight of her. He was still stunned by her gentle beauty, the long, flowing, brown hair and those seductive, but somehow conniving blue eyes. If the work permitted it, Garrett would often just stare at her while doing his chores. He sometimes felt that he, too, was being watched. At first he thought it was a case of nerves for it was a feeling he often had had during the war. Then one day, he confirmed that she was glancing furtively at him when it was unlikely he would catch her. He had discovered her secret glances as he was re-arranging a shelf and his eyes met hers in a mirror. Although he couldn't say for sure, he thought she blushed upon being caught. Garrett smiled to himself and let the moment pass, relieved that she was not totally oblivious to his presence.

As for Peggy Dobbs, she was intrigued by Morgan Garrett, former Confederate soldier, a species that she had heard her father rail against in times past and the species which had killed her brother. Peggy had known other Confederates, since several of the boys her age in Madden County had fought for the South, but they were ones she had lived around and known. Here was Garrett, a Confederate she had been unacquainted with until two weeks ago and still she knew very little of his past. He piqued her curiosity, much like a wrapped package stirs a child. Further, she had a maternal compassion for him because of the lame arm. She could not figure why he never buttoned the cuff on the sleeve of his good hand. Were it not for that withered limb, he would be a handsome man. That was what she had been thinking the day his eyes met hers in the mirror, and that was why she blushed.

Garrett's work at the Dobbs General Store offered the first challenge in adjusting to his one-armed existence. Since the war ended, he had done no work until reaching Cross-rock. His life had consisted mostly of moving westward. The greatest chore had first been in saddling and unsaddling his chestnut, but Garrett managed that, helped by his light Jenifer model cavalry saddle. But here, each day seemed to present a new challenge to him. Like the first day he dusted the shelves when he had nothing else to do. Such a simple chore with two good hands becomes a trial with just one. With two hands Garrett could have picked up the box of soap or tin of tobacco and dusted under it. With one good hand, though, he had to move the object, put it down, pick up the duster, dust, set the duster aside and then replace the merchandise.

Most things in the store Garrett learned to handle with no great problem. If he could get a good hold on it, he could move it because the strength of his right arm seemed to be increasing to accommodate the infirmity of his left one. The fifty-pound sacks and some of the other cumbersome goods offered a greater challenge, but after several tries, Garrett worked out a system that allowed him to maneuver them wherever needed.

But the one thing Garrett always felt silly doing was the sweeping. With two hands and arms, it is such a simple chore that it requires no thought. With only one good limb, however, it becomes much more of a test. Not that it was impossible, but with the broom held in his right hand and tucked under his good arm, Garrett knew he looked foolish hunkered over the floor, swaying with the broom over an ever growing pile of debris.

One afternoon when Dobbs was out of the store and Garrett was sweeping up, Brad Decker entered the building. Garrett had been sweeping near the front with his back to the door. When the bells on the knob were disturbed from their peace, Garrett turned and found himself face-to-face with Decker. Peggy, at her accustomed place, stopped her reading and watched the encounter.

"Well, if it isn't old Lefty," Decker sneered with his cutting reference to Garrett's bad arm. "How do you like doing girl's work?"

"It's honest work which is more than most

57

around here say about your occupation. Have you business here or did you just come to pay your respects?"

"Business, of course, but I'll let the girl take care of me. She can probably get it done twice as fast as you, Lefty."

Garrett stood there a moment just looking Decker over and not liking what he saw. Those two small scars that ran parallel down Decker's right cheek caught Garrett's gray eyes again and he wondered about the mystery behind them. Then, ignoring the brown-eyed stare of Decker, Garrett resumed his chore with an exaggerated gusto that reflected his own pride and his refusal to be intimidated by a two-fisted thug. Decker, for his part in the encounter, noticed a change in Garrett. Those gray eyes, which had been listless and dull during their first encounter, were now bright and belligerent. It was a look Decker knew to be dangerous, but coming from a one-armed man, Decker found himself amused.

"Peg," said Decker, turning to the girl, "get me a couple pounds of coffee. Seems you're the only place around that has any genuine coffee."

She got up from her chair and silently began filling the order. The exchange between Decker and Garrett had made her even more uncomfortable in her father's absence. She had always been uneasy around him and hated to encounter Decker on the street. As probably the most eligible woman in Crossrock, Peggy had been the fancy of most of the town's young men. But with Decker, it was different, at least from outward appearances. That was what worried her about Decker. His near lack of interest seemed dangerous, as if he had sinister designs on her. Events during the war had heightened those fears even more, and now as she fetched the coffee she was glad for Garrett's presence. It was a tacit admission to herself, at first, that she was glad her father had hired Garrett. Had she a choice, she would have preferred Billy Murphy to be there with his two good strong arms. However, in his absence, Peggy was glad for Garrett.

In paying for the coffee, Decker pulled from his pocket a wad of bills unlike any Garrett had seen in Crossrock. The money roll confirmed in Garrett's mind that what the others had said about Decker was true. No one who did anything honest for a living would have that kind of money — not in Crossrock, not this year.

"Good to see you, Peg," he said. "You're just as talkative as ever."

Turning from the counter with his bag of coffee, Decker made sure he walked right through the pile of dust and trash that Garrett had swept up.

"See you again, Lefty," he said with a laugh. "Keep up the good work."

Out the door he went and Garrett stopped his sweeping and watched him as he crossed the street to the abandoned boarding house, then walked down the opposite plank sidewalk and disappeared from view in the store window.

"Some friend you have there," Garrett said, turning to Peggy Dobbs.

"He's no friend of mine. Few people like a bully and that's probably the nicest thing anyone would ever say about him."

"How did he get those two scars on his cheek?"

"That's a question a lot of people around these parts would like answered. He turned up with them about two years ago during the war. It was at about the same time a young woman, a Mrs. Dawson, and her two girls were found murdered south of here on North Fork Creek. Some said it was Comanches, but there wasn't any other Indian trouble this far east then. Others said it was Decker and his boys. Seems they were the ones that found her and buried her and the

60

two girls. No one else ever saw the bodies so they had to take Decker's word."

"Who do you believe did it?"

"Probably Decker. We might have known had Mr. Dawson returned from the war, because he loved her and those girls and he would have found out. But he died at Jenkins Ferry and there was no one else who would have risked running afoul of Decker over it, since it wasn't their kin that was killed."

"Seems this Decker is on the minds of a lot of people around here when they've got enough to worry about just in starting over."

"It's true," said Peggy, as she seated herself and resumed her silent reading.

Garrett was pleased that she had at least answered his questions with more than the curt responses that he had grown used to. But he realized that her elaborate response was more a result of her obvious uneasiness around Decker than a thawing of her attitude toward him. Nonetheless, he was pleased.

Peggy, too, was pleased, but her relief was in getting back to her book which provided the wall that helped her keep a measured distance from Garrett. He made her nervous, but it was a different, less physically frightening way than Decker. But in another way, an emotional way, Garrett was more troubling. The book helped her ignore those fears.

"Father," Peggy said, as soon as Dobbs returned, "Brad Decker was here while you were gone."

"Any trouble?"

"Well, he and Mr. Garrett did have an exchange of words."

"Anything to it?" asked Dobbs, turning to Garrett.

"Nothing. Just an ornery streak that I have seen in a few other men in recent years."

"Well, you be careful around that man. You remember that you don't have two good arms anymore, you hear?"

"Decker won't let me forget that," said Garrett.

"It's true," interjected Peggy. "He kept calling Mr. Garrett 'Lefty.' "

"That's Decker, all right, a nice word for everybody. What'd he want in here anyway?"

"Just some coffee," answered Peggy.

"He was carrying a pretty good roll of money," said Garrett. "How'd he come up with that? Any idea?"

"Folks around here have got a lot of ideas, but no proof," said Dobbs with his furrowed brow.

The furrowed brow, Garrett had learned,

meant Dobbs was serious. His face always frowned, due to the absence of all his upper teeth except the front four. As a result, Garrett had had to learn what the clue was on his disposition since the continual frown meant nothing. The wrinkled forehead was the key.

"You know during the war a lot of things either didn't get done or got out of hand. Most of the farming didn't get done, but those that had cattle found their herds increasing without attention. With no honest men here to keep tallies and to brand their own stock, a lot ran free.

"Some say," Dobbs continued, "that Decker and his boys appropriated some of that stock and then sold the cattle elsewhere. Others say, that some of the unexplained happenings around here were a result of Decker's band. There was the killing of Mrs. Dawson and her two girls which . . ."

"Your daughter told me about that," Garrett interrupted.

"That and just a lot of other things didn't add up. And every time something did happen, Decker always had too good an alibi. Then again, none of us old men were going to question him."

"I guess not," said Garrett, realizing that the lame arm had done to him the same thing that age had accomplished with Dobbs and his friends. For a moment Garrett felt old and useless, just half a man. Then that pride, the pride which had caught Decker's attention, took control. In that moment of self-pity and then prideful redemption, Garrett vowed to himself that he would not be cowered by Decker and his gang of ruffians. He had ridden against hundreds during the war and would not be intimidated by a handful of men too cowardly to enlist in the army. If death were the alternative, heaven or hell couldn't be any rougher for a one-armed man than trying to make a living in Texas.

In the days following his vow, Garrett felt more at ease with himself and more confident of his capabilities than at any time since he was wounded in Virginia. By then, the job was routine. He was up early enough to wash in the basin in the back room with his meager belongings and to dress before Dobbs arrived. Every morning at seven o'clock he greeted Dobbs as the old man came to work. At eight o'clock, the two of them unlocked the front door and opened up for business. Garrett always looked forward to nine o'clock because that was when Peggy Dobbs came from the house to the store. Each day he awaited her arrival with the anticipation of a young boy eager for school to be dismissed. Her quiet presence could make even the coldest day warmer for Garrett. On days she wore the yellow blouse with the buttoned-up collar, he was especially pleased. That was what she wore the first glance he ever had of her and it remained his favorite.

Peggy Dobbs had also changed her mind about Garrett. Her obstinacy prevented her from admitting that perhaps her father was right in hiring the Alabaman. Ever since her father had given Garrett a pair of used, but otherwise good, trousers and a new shirt to wear around the store, Peggy had not seen him so much as an ex-Confederate soldier, but as a gentleman of the South. He was always courteous to her and she liked that. Her indifference had turned to a tolerance that was only strained when Garrett would leave the store in cold weather and wear his long, gray overcoat for cover. She did not like that coat because it reminded her that her father had hired him over her objections. That part of her resentment lingered, although time was gradually gnawing away even that. Despite her gradual shift in demeanor toward Garrett, she still used the books to preserve that one barrier that separated him and her from the normal small talk usually shared by co-workers.

To her it was always a comfort when Billy Murphy was around the store. With him she felt safe, comfortable. His strong arms and large frame made Murphy an impressive man physically and the only fear his presence never seemed to allay was the one she had of Decker. Murphy's looks were rather common and seldom impressed people either with handsomeness or ugliness. Instead, it was the massive build that people remembered. Only later did they take in that man's ruddy complexion, red hair and steady green eyes. Billy Murphy had not yet asked Peggy to marry him, but she knew he would. Of the men she could have chosen from, Billy was not the handsomest, but he was the most dependable and probably the hardest working. Those were traits that weren't always found in the literature she read, but they were qualities she had grown to demand. That was something Peggy's mother had taught her when she used to work beside her husband at the store.

"Look at your father," Mrs. Dobbs would say. "See how he works? He's always busy and it means he is always thinking about his family. A husband who does that is solid, and whatever faults he may have will be tempered by that strength. You look at men and you'll see."

Peggy had listened to her mother, who promised to give her daughter the wedding dress in which she had married Dobbs, and it was advice she heeded well. Whether by choice or by mere repetition, she did not know. Billy Murphy fit well her mother's criteria. Like her father, Murphy cared little for the books which preoccupied Peggy. But Peggy, never giving thought to her mother's failure to do so with her father, knew she could interest Murphy in books once they were married. It wouldn't be hard, she thought.

Murphy had ambitions to be the biggest farmer in Madden County, Texas one day. It was a drive that kept him busy when others around Crossrock used the cold weather as an excuse to slow down their work. Having fought for the Union was, of course, an advantage for Murphy's ambitions because he had been paid when the war was over, and the money was still good. He put some money aside, possibly for marriage, and used some of the rest to buy a hundred acres of good land along the North Fork about two miles south of town. Since purchasing the land he had spent a great deal of time getting rid of the mesquite bushes and stones that blemished his would-be fields.

Realizing that just getting his fields ready for planting did nothing to bring in money until next year, Murphy had put his mind to figuring out how to increase his nest egg. The idea came to him one day after Dobbs had asked him if he would chop and haul in some firewood to the store. There was little timber of any type within convenient distance of Crossrock. However, about eight miles to the north was Four Corners, a wooded canyon spot named for a log cabin that had been started there but never finished. The country around Four Corners was rough land — mountains with flat tops and an obstacle course of gulleys and crevices which were normally dry. With his shotgun at his side and an ax in the back of his wagon, Murphy rode to Four Corners once a week for a day of chopping firewood. In Crossrock, he found a suitable market from the old men, war widows and a few stores, including Dobbs's and the Benton Saloon. When he wasn't paid in cash, he accepted IOUs and meals or bartered for some tools which might help him around the rough cabin on his farm. The cabin was not the kind of home a fellow would bring a new wife to live, so Murphy was intent on waiting until after his crops were harvested next year to propose marriage. Then, he thought, he would have the time and enough money to build a house more suited to the delicate needs of Peggy Dobbs.

It was on one of those unseasonably warm afternoons, which occasionally disrupted the winter weather in Crossrock, that Bill Murphy came to town with a wagonload of wood to sell. He had unloaded some of his best firewood behind the Dobbs General Store, but had done the task so quietly that no one in the store realized he was in town until he pulled his wagon around in front of the building. Jumping off his wagon, Murphy strode into the store with those massive arms swinging with each step.

"You've got a two-week supply of firewood stacked in back, Mr. Dobbs," said Murphy. "It'll supply you longer if this warm weather keeps up."

"Good work, Bill. Did you leave any at the house?"

"Not yet," replied Murphy. "I've got to make a delivery at Benton's. Thought I would stop there first, then make yours the final stop."

"Get there about supper time, eh?"

"It had entered my mind," said Bill.

"Okay, Peggy, you heard him so fix enough

extra for Bill here."

Peggy just smiled with a touch of coyness and nodded her head. Eying Murphy as he left the store, she breathed contentedly as he climbed into the seat of his wagon and moved his team to the front of the Benton Saloon.

The Bentons had their firewood stacked by the side door rather than in back of the saloon. Since the space between the saloon and the neighboring vacant building was too narrow to get a wagon through, Murphy had to stop his team on the street and carry the wood some twenty feet to stack it.

With his usual vigor, Murphy began the chore of carrying armloads of firewood between the buildings and replenishing the dwindling Benton supply. Concentrating more on his work and thinking of his supper date at the Dobbs's house, Murphy never noticed Decker and his four companions converging toward his wagon. As Murphy climbed into the back to get another load of wood, one of Decker's companions saw the opportunity for a little more fun. Picking up a stone as Murphy gathered another bundle of wood, the miscreant let out an Indian scream and threw the rock, hitting one of Murphy's horses in the flank.

Startled by the commotion and the sting

of the well-aimed stone, the horse bolted down the street, throwing Murphy from the wagon. Murphy hit the ground with a thud, his huge frame making the earth shudder. Realizing what had happened when he saw Decker and his pals laughing at his expense, Murphy let out a curdling yell and bounced up to attack. By chance he picked out the stone thrower as his immediate target. Catching the surprised man around the waist, Murphy picked him up and tossed him a good ten feet.

That was when the laughing stopped. As the downed man got up, Murphy made another charge at him, knocking the fellow into the dirt again. Reacting to the plight of their companion, Decker and the other three ruffians circled Murphy before he could reach the downed man a third time. Murphy was not overawed for he began grabbing at the other four as well. Against two or three, Murphy had the strength to hold his own, if not to claim a total victory. But against five, it was a standoff. Every time Murphy grabbed for one of his antagonists, another two of them would jump on his back, knocking him off stride or breaking his hold.

Back at the Dobbs General Store, Peggy heard the yell at her reading post near the window. Looking out the window to investigate, she saw Murphy in trouble.

"Father, father," she screamed. "They're roughing up Billy."

Instantly, Garrett, who had been stocking shelves, jumped off the stool he was standing on and ran out into the street. There he saw Murphy, encircled and clawing at his attackers like a coon surrounded by hounds.

Garrett flew down the street, reaching the crowd just as Murphy made another lunge at his tormentors. This time Murphy succeeded in grabbing one. As the others converged on Murphy, pummeling him with their fists, the massive redheaded man used all his might to squeeze the breath from his captive, but his strength was being sapped by the blows of the others.

Garrett, knowing he could not handle the other four men with his good hand, spied a club-shaped piece of firewood on the ground. Grabbing it, he rushed the swirling circle and struck the first head that came within range. Now there was one less to worry about. Instantly, though, Garrett found himself beset by two of the men who had turned their attention in his direction. That moment of reprieve allowed Murphy to cast away his breathless captive and wrestle his only remaining tormentor to the

72

ground where he bloodied the man's face with a flurry of punches, all of which struck the target.

Although Murphy's fortunes had improved with Garrett's arrival, Garrett found his own situation had worsened. He was being stalked like a lame animal by Decker and his remaining ally. They circled Garrett and both ran at him at once. Garrett's swings with the wooden club were useless. Suddenly he was held from behind and straightened up for Decker, who delivered a blow to the stomach. Garrett, doubled over by the impact, kept his senses despite the pain. As he was raised for another blow, he kicked Decker a glancing blow to the stomach. The kick inflicted little pain to Decker, but did increase his rage. He approached Garrett, who was still in the grips of the second henchman, more cautiously. Swinging for the head, Decker smashed Garrett on the cheek with a bloody accuracy that left him stunned on the ground.

Just as Decker was preparing to deliver a final crushing blow with all his vindictive might, Murphy jumped up from his immobilized victim and tackled Decker. The two exchanged frightful punches with Decker, surprisingly, holding his own against the huge Murphy. While Garrett and his opponent were still struggling, the thug the Alabaman had first knocked out came to. Seeing the plight of Decker, he began to pull his pistol from its holster. Just as Murphy knocked Decker to the ground, a shot rang out and dust flew in front of the gunman's feet.

"Put that gun back in the holster!" yelled saloonkeeper Benton, standing on the walk in front of his saloon with a smoking shotgun in his hand.

The shotgun blast had struck no one, but it brought a halt to the fight as quickly as if every participant had been wounded.

"You boys have had your fun," Benton went on, "and I don't want things to get out of hand, not while I've still got firewood to be unloaded. Brad, you and your friends move on out and leave these two alone."

"Let's go boys," sulked Decker, who was wise enough to know there was no way to win an argument with a double-barreled shotgun, "some fellows just don't enjoy our fun."

Then, looking from Murphy to Garrett, Decker continued, "The next time we meet things aren't going to be for fun. We intend to get you for this. Lefty, we were just having fun 'til you butted in. We won't forget."

"That sounds like a threat you'd better

reconsider," said Garrett.

"No threat," said Decker. "Just some friendly advice, Lefty."

The five men slowly walked away from the scene of their encounter. Decker was bleeding from the mouth. One man had a knot on the back of his head. Another was still gasping for breath and still another had a face that was a bloody mess. Only the one who had grabbed Garrett from behind had emerged unscathed.

Murphy had some bruises, but no blood was spilled. Garrett, meanwhile, looked pitiful with blood streaming from his nose and staining his clothes.

"Thanks," said Murphy. "I owe you one."

Maude Benton ran out of the saloon with a towel in her hands and headed straight for Garrett. Peggy, too, came racing down the street, her brown hair blowing as she ran. She hugged Murphy when she reached him.

"Are you okay?"

"Yeah, nothing serious. Just a little bit sore."

"And you?" she inquired, turning to Garrett.

"A bit messy, but nothing else the matter."

"If you're okay, Garrett," said Murphy, "I'm gonna fetch my team and finish up my delivery here. Then I am going to be ready for a good supper."

Murphy left Garrett with Peggy and Maude Benton.

"I told you those boys were troublemakers," Maude Benton lectured. "You've got to be more careful from now on because they are sure to come after you."

"He don't need no lecture," said her husband. "He knows what they said and he'll manage right fine without you repeating everything."

"It's okay," said Garrett, whose nose had stopped bleeding.

The two women and Benton helped Garrett to his feet. Although he was capable of rising on his own, when he saw that Peggy was going to help him he malingered just to feel her touch. Since they had never even shaken hands before, Garrett enjoyed her warm hand clasped around his wrist. As he stood, he acted a bit weak.

"Are you sure you can make it back to the store?" asked Maude Benton.

"I think so," he responded.

Nonetheless, Peggy grabbed him by the arm and assisted him back to the store. It was the best medicine Garrett could think of.

"That was a courageous thing you did to

help Billy," said Peggy softly as they walked back to the store.

"Courage mounts with the occasion," answered Garrett without a thought of where he had picked up that saying.

"Shakespeare, isn't it?"

"Isn't what?"

"That line 'courage mounteth with occasion.' Isn't that Shakespeare?"

"I don't remember," said Garrett. "I guess I did read it somewhere, but I don't know. I can't remember for sure."

"Did you ever read any Shakespeare?" inquired Peggy with mounting interest.

"When I went to the academy, I had to read a lot of things, including a little Shakespeare."

"Really, I bet you're the only man within a hundred miles of here that's read him. Don't you enjoy it?"

"Been a while since I read him. I must not enjoy him as much as you because I'm not reading a book every waking moment of the day."

"Nor do I, nor do I," she responded.

Her father was waiting for Garrett and Peggy outside his store on the wooden walk.

"You okay?" asked Dobbs when Garrett reached him.

"I think so. Just a little bloody, I guess."

"Well, why don't you go on in the back and change into your old clothes. I'll have Peggy wash those you've got on."

Garrett did as he was told and then rejoined Dobbs and Peggy in the store front.

"Why don't you join us for supper tonight," Dobbs said. "I'm sure a good hot meal would help you get over those bruises a little faster. Peggy, why don't you go on and get started on supper. And fix plenty 'cause Bill eats enough for three and I'm sure Morgan here is pretty well famished too."

Dobbs waited until Peggy had gathered Garrett's bloody clothes and then continued.

"I guess you know the Decker boys will be out to get you and Bill. From now on you've got to be extra careful. Keep that gun of yours loaded and ready to use and don't leave this store without taking it along."

"That's the third warning I've had in the last hour. People around here sure run scared of Decker and his bunch."

"It's a matter of self-preservation. We haven't had a sheriff since '63 and we've got no one else to turn to. We're just trying to survive, that's all. Tonight when you come over, I want you to bring your gun."

"You're the boss."

"It's getting about closing time. Let's get things put away and covered up. Then why don't you come over about seven-thirty."

"I'll try, but I am not sure I will make it on time."

"Why not?"

"I don't have a watch."

Dobbs pulled out his gold pocket watch. He looked at it almost tenderly. Then, after almost putting it back in his pocket, Dobbs handed it to Garrett.

"Use this," he said. "It keeps good time and just bring it with you when you come."

With that, Dobbs turned and went out the door, locking Garrett in.

Garrett fingered the watch carefully. The plain gold case was decorated only with an embossed "D," but the cover had been dented slightly through the center, making the letter look as much like a "B" as a "D." Garrett looked at the time. He had better than an hour so he went into his room and rested, thinking about the events of the day. His thoughts dwelled not so much on the fight, but on the touch of Peggy, the conversation with her and the chance to join her for supper. That made up for the aches and pains of his bruised body and his swollen face.

CHAPTER 4

"You look just awful," said Peggy Dobbs after opening the door to her home sharply at seven-thirty and finding Garrett.

It was not the type of welcome Garrett had expected, but, then again, Garrett realized he hadn't looked at himself in a mirror and his face did ache from the fight. Speechless, he just stood there in the doorway of the four-room house and stared at Peggy.

"Well, come in, come in unless you want me to ruin our supper."

Garrett walked into the house with an exaggerated pace brought on by the girl's scolding. Seated in a rocking chair was Dobbs, relaxing with the somnolent motion of the rocker. Murphy, too, was present, his large body taking up half the couch.

"Take off your hat and join us, Morgan," said Dobbs. "We were just talking about the little altercation this afternoon. Your participation in that brawl is certainly evident."

Seating himself across from Dobbs and Murphy, Garrett agreed, "If it looks like it feels it must be pretty bad. I don't know how Murphy managed to come out looking so clean. As big as he is, it wasn't for their lack of a target."

"Ha," laughed Dobbs, "that's a good one. I don't know either, but Bill here always seems to come out unscratched. He went through the war without getting so much as a nick. Even that time he fell off the roof of the store when he was cleaning out the stovepipe, he got up and climbed back to finish the chore. He didn't break a bone."

"I've just been lucky, though it does help to be on the right side," said Murphy.

"Now, let's not get into politics," Dobbs broke in, "because that's where you were heading with your talk, Bill. The war's over now and let's try to forget it. There are always good men on both sides of a big dispute and I'm sitting in a room with a couple good men. I don't care what side they fought on."

Following the reprimand, there was a lull in the conversation and Garrett could hear Peggy, busily preparing supper in the kitchen behind him. As he listened to her, he gazed around the sitting room. In addition to the rocker, the couch and the chair he was seated in, there were two small tables with lamps atop them, a large chest and, against the far wall, a bookshelf larger than the one in the backroom of the store. Peggy did indeed have a good library to choose from.

"I guess you boys realize that you must be on your guard now," said Dobbs in resuming the conversation.

The perpetual frown on Dobbs's face seemed more pronounced than Garrett had ever noticed. The brow was more deeply furrowed. Dobbs was truly worried or scared.

"No good has ever come to anyone that tangles with Decker and his boys. You are going to have to stay alert. Where's your sidearm, Morgan?"

"I forgot it," said Garrett sheepishly.

"If you want to keep your job, you'd better keep that gun with you. When I hired you, I told you I wanted that gun for the protection of my store. Now I want it for your own protection as well. Bill, I know you keep your shotgun handy, but you'd better keep a sidearm with you, too. You can get whatever ammunition you need at the store and you'd better do it. Do you two understand?"

"Yes, sir," they replied in unplanned military unison.

"Bill, how many more trips are you going to need to make to Four Corners to have enough wood stockpiled for your customers?"

"Probably four or five," Murphy answered.

"Don't go alone. I am going to see that Morgan goes with you because I don't want you waylaid. He can keep a watch out while you do your chopping."

Neither Garrett nor Murphy relished that forced companionship, but they knew it was foolish to try to argue with Dobbs now that his mind was set. Garrett, knowing only about Decker of the five potential adversaries, asked Dobbs and Murphy about the other four.

Murphy did most of the talking. One, the man who had grabbed Garrett from behind and walked away from the fight unharmed, was named Ed Skinner. Lucky Ed, they called him. Tall and lanky, Skinner had grown up in Madden County, but never had been liked by most because he was always in trouble. When not involved in mischief of one type or another, he could usually be found drinking, either at the saloon or out on the street.

The man who had started the fight by

spooking Murphy's team first appeared around Crossrock about the time most of the county's young men had been going east to fight the war. His name was not known, but people, including his companions, called him Snuff because there was always a trail of the tobacco running from the corner of his mouth down his black beard.

The other two were brothers. Willie Norman was the one that Murphy had squeezed almost to death. A stumpy, unkempt fellow, Willie Norman had been accused of stealing horses in Flores County, but he had never been brought to trial. Selmer Norman was Willie's kid brother. Had Selmer had a law-abiding brother, he might have been a good citizen himself. But he was a follower, and from the day he was born he copied the felonious ways of Willie. Physically, though, Selmer's tall and lean frame was a direct opposite to his older brother's stumpy body.

"They're a motley group," concluded Murphy. "Not a one of them, save possibly Selmer, with a bit of decency. I always thought Selmer would have turned out all right had he not admired Willie so. Whatever, though, you can't trust any of them."

The aromas from the kitchen began to distract the conversation and it wasn't long before Peggy called the trio to supper.

"It's ready. Anybody hungry?" she yelled.

Murphy jumped from his seat and led the other two less agile men into the kitchen. They sat down and began to help themselves. It was a good meal. Peggy had fixed chicken and dumplings with dried beans, potato cakes and fresh bread. Garrett enjoyed himself thoroughly for this was the first good evening meal he had eaten in weeks. Usually, he would take lunch at the Benton Saloon and then do without much at night. Since that was still more than the war rations he had lived on the previous four years, Garrett had actually gained back some of his weight from the single daily meal. However, it was good to top a day off with a warm meal rather than a few store crackers, his normal evening fare of late. Garrett's mealtime enthusiasm kept him on a helping-for-helping par with Murphy.

"Shame you boys don't enjoy a meal," Dobbs laughed, as they finished every morsel on the table.

Pushing himself away from the table and stretching out, Garrett remembered Dobbs's watch was in the pocket of his shirt. Pulling the watch out, he reached across the table to return it to Dobbs.

"Thanks for loaning me your watch."

"You loaned him Tom's watch?" asked Peggy with the look of subdued anger that Garrett had not seen since the day he was hired. "You loaned it to someone who wore gray?"

"That's right," replied Dobbs, "I let him use it and I'll do it again, if he asks. You didn't see anybody else in town come to Bill's side this afternoon and help him. You owe him a few thanks, don't you think?"

"But Tom's watch? That's all you have of Tom's. Are you forgetting he was killed by a man in gray?"

"What Morgan wears now is just clothes," said the father, his brow creased again. "It doesn't matter if it is gray because it's no longer a uniform. That changed the day the war was over."

Dobbs's eyes began to cloud and Garrett could read in them a deep longing for his son. But Garrett envied Dobbs in a way. At least the old man had gotten to see his son grown. Garrett once had two sons, young sons. At the ages of six and four years, both had died of cholera along with their mother. It was the loss of his family more than the loss of his land that had prompted Garrett to leave his Alabama home and head west. And even in this remote Texas town, Garrett was faced with the inevitability of never being able to escape those haunting memories.

"I know it must have been painful to lose your son," Garrett began, but Murphy interrupted.

"How can you know? Tom lost his life to a yellow-bellied, gray-coated sniper. There wasn't a better man in Madden County and he died in my arms. I took that watch from his warm body to return to his family. It's more than just a watch to us. That's all we have left of him."

"Hush," shouted Dobbs, "Morgan is a guest in my home, just as you are a guest, Bill. I will have no more outbreaks like that, not when this man helped you out of a tight spot today."

"Just the same," said Murphy, "Peggy's right about lending him the watch."

Dobbs, his rage equaled only by the frustration his simple gesture had created, arose from the table.

"Come on Morgan, let's go into the front room for a while."

Garrett followed Dobbs into the sitting room and reoccupied the chair he had taken when he arrived. The old man began to talk about his dead son. It was not the watch that bothered Peggy and Bill, he told Garrett, but the loss of Tom. Bill and Tom had been the best of friends from their child-

87

hood in Indiana until Tom's death.

Tom's dying like he did in Bill's arms had been a devastating blow to Murphy. There was now a bitterness in Murphy that was not there before the war. Tom's death, however, was most damaging on the boy's mother. Despondent over the death, she seemed to lose her own will to live. One morning about six months after Tom's death, Dobbs said he awoke to find his wife dead in bed beside him. The loss of her brother and mother so close together had shaken Peggy badly. Always a bookworm, Peggy had retreated further into her books and had lost the vivaciousness that had long been her character.

"I probably don't have many years left either," whispered Dobbs, who did not want to be heard in the kitchen, "and Peggy is unprepared to face the world by herself, no matter what she thinks. I've had to try and get her over the past so it won't alienate her from her future."

"It must be hard," nodded Garrett.

"It is, it is. That's another reason I hired you — thinking maybe if she could be around somebody that was decent and had fought on the other side from Tom, she would snap out of this. I haven't been successful, thus far though."

Bill and Peggy had remained in the kitchen after supper, preferring a little privacy to a conversation with Garrett. When they did not reappear before Garrett decided it was time to go back to the store, Dobbs called for them to say goodbye. They did so unenthusiastically. Garrett left the house and stepped into a cold wind that came in from the north. He knew he would need to fire up the stove when he got back to the store, although all his aching body really wanted was some rest. A lot had happened in the last eight hours and Garrett found it hard to sort things out. He thought that he had won the respect of Murphy and Peggy after pitching in during the fight, but even that was now uncertain. After the words over the watch, he guessed the situation was like the weather — just too unpredictable to ever understand.

Garrett slept so soundly that night that he was not up when Dobbs came in to open up the next morning. Only the ringing of the bells on the door awoke Garrett from his slumber, and then he was embarrassed to find Dobbs staring in on him.

"Looks like you overslept a little."

"I reckon so. An aching body, a full stomach and cold weather will do that to you."

Hastily, Garrett got dressed in his gray clothes and began his daily routine, but something was out of the ordinary. At mid-morning he realized that Peggy had yet to come in.

"Where's Peggy? She ill?"

"Not at all. I told her this morning that she owed you an apology and that didn't set well with her. She got even madder when I told her that I wanted her to wash those bloody clothes of yours and get them back to you today. I suspect the washing will delay her until late afternoon. It's hard to get clothes dry on a day as cold as this."

About an hour before closing time, which was normally when Peggy would go home to fix supper for her father, she came to the store. In her arms were the neatly folded trousers and shirt which Dobbs had given Garrett to wear around the store.

"Here are your clothes," she said. "Father wanted me to get them cleaned up and back to you today."

"Thank you. It was kind of you to do it."

Garrett looked into her blue eyes, trying to read her thoughts. The anger in them had dissipated, but he could discern no other sign about her disposition. Slowly, Garrett was coming to the conclusion that no matter what he did, she would forever maintain toward him that cold cordiality which he so wanted to change.

"Thank you," he said once more as he took the clothes and carried them into the back room. The ringing of the bells on the door told him that Peggy would not be there when he returned to the front.

The next morning Peggy, book in hand, returned to the store at the regular time, an hour after opening. She seemed nervous because she fidgeted over her book as she sat by the window. Her uneasiness would have made Garrett restless had he not been busy with several customers, some who bought and some who just came in for the warmth and the conversation. Peggy was wearing her yellow blouse, Garrett's favorite, but he had not even noticed with all the activity in the store. Kids looked enviously at what candy was available. Men covetously handled some of the leather goods, firearms or tools. And the women — they longed for the gingham or calico, or for the fancy lace. Those things were what the people wanted to buy. What they actually bought, though, was more flour, more beans, perhaps a little salt and a little com meal. Then it was back home for them, the trip to the store their entertainment for the day.

For a morning that had been so busy, the

afternoon was positively slow. About mid-afternoon, Dobbs left to run some errands and Garrett was then alone with Peggy for the first time since the fight. He had expected her to remain seated and quiet, so he was surprised when she spoke.

"Have you ever read Shakespeare's *Merchant of Venice?*"

"I don't recall for sure," replied Garrett.

"Well, I have been reading it. Funny how these things work out, but I started it the day of the fight. It's made me think, though, and I guess that I owe you an apology. Father kept telling me that I should apologize to you, but I am a bit stubborn on these things. Then, too, Shakespeare has a way of saying things that Father never approaches. Listen to this."

Peggy opened the book she had fidgeted over all day. She stopped at a page near the end of the volume. Then she began to read:

The quality of mercy is not strain'd
It droppeth as the gentle rain from heaven
Upon the place beneath: it is twice blest;
It blesseth him that gives, and him that
   takes:
'Tis mightiest in the mightiest: it becomes
The throned monarch better than his crown;

His sceptre shows the force of temporal
    power,
The attribute to awe and majesty,
Wherein doth sit the dread and fear of
    kings;
But mercy is above this sceptred sway;
It is enthroned in the hearts of kings,
It is an attribute to God himself;
And earthly power doth then show likest
    God's
When mercy season justice.

Pausing after finishing the passage, she lifted her blue eyes until they met Garrett's gray eyes.

"It's beautiful isn't it? I guess the quality of my mercy toward you has been very poor. I know you didn't kill Tom, but your gray uniform has made me resent you. You have been an honorable gentleman in my presence and I thank you. I am grateful, too, for you helping Billy out the other day when there was no one else to do it. Do you think you can forgive me?"

Garrett raced through his mind for something of Shakespeare's that he could answer affirmatively with, but his mind came up blank. Instead of something eloquent, Garrett responded simply.

"Sure, it would please me greatly to forget

about it. After all, we do work in the same store and are together a big part of the day."

"Okay then, that is done," she said. "But there is one other thing. It's about the watch. One reason I was mad the other night at supper was because I was shocked. When Bill returned from the war with that watch and gave it to Father, Father just broke down. I had never seen him like that before. He was so upset. He took Tom's death better than Mother or me. But that watch really brought home to him the loss of Tom and he just cried. He swore then that he would never let go of that watch. Many times I have seen him take that watch from his pocket, look at the time and just stand there, holding it reverently.

"It just shocked me," she continued, "when I saw that he had loaned it to you. At first, I resented it because I thought he had forgotten Tom, but then maybe he had just accepted it better. I want you to know that I am sorry I took it the way I did."

"I regret it happened too," said Garrett. "It was such an innocent gesture, him loaning me the watch, that I never thought about it until I gave it back to him. Then I was sorry I had accepted it."

"Don't be. It's just one of those things

that happen and maybe it was for the better."

"Is Murphy still mad about it?"

"Probably," replied Peggy. "He never forgets things, but after a while he usually gets over it. He is stubborner than me."

"I don't know about that, but he is certainly not as pretty as you."

Peggy blushed and Garrett knew he had made her uncomfortable for the first time since their eyes had met in the mirror that day. Quickly, he decided to change the subject to her book.

"Seems like I remember reading *The Merchant of Venice*," he said, and her face immediately brightened. "Isn't it the one where the young maiden is being courted by several suitors? Before her father will give permission for anyone to marry her, the suitor must pick from a golden, silver or leaden cask, one of which has her likeness inside?"

"That's it," she smiled approvingly.

"Then one of my favorite lines of Shakespeare is in that play."

"Oh, tell me what it is."

"Well, you remember when one of those suitors opened up the wrong box, he spoke my favorite line: 'Oh, Hell!' "

"That's scandalous," gasped Peggy in

mock anger.

"It may be," said Garrett, chuckling, "but it's still Shakespeare."

"You're impossible. If that's all the Shakespeare you know, it's just enough to make a fool of yourself."

"And you, too," he said, the chuckle becoming open laughter.

"Oh, you," she shrugged, "I knew I should have continued to read my book."

But instead of returning to her chair and finishing her reading, she put on an apron, a first since Garrett had arrived. With that she began to move about the store straightening up as only a woman can. And Garrett, in a reversal of roles merely stood behind the counter and watched the fluid motions of the woman as she scurried from place to place, singing softly. It was then that he finally noticed she was wearing his favorite yellow blouse. She was beautiful, he thought. How he wished for two good arms, so maybe then Peggy would see him as more than just a lame storekeeper.

When Dobbs returned from his errands, he could tell that Peggy and Garrett had made their peace. He was pleased because he liked Garrett, liked him ever since the first day he walked into the store. There was something about him, perhaps his straightforward approach or his calm demeanor, that reminded Dobbs of his dead son. Dobbs had not realized it then, but one reason he hired Garrett was that he did resemble Tom in some very subtle ways. Garrett's presence had a serene effect on Dobbs. Even his crippled arm seemed to add to the man's strength, Dobbs thought. His presence was a blessing to the store owner. There was no one else, not even Bill Murphy, to whom Dobbs would have loaned Tom's watch; and he would do it again, despite the objections of Bill and Peggy, if the occasion arose.

The moment Dobbs returned, Garrett noticed a strange, peaceful look on the man's face. And, for the first time, Garrett saw a crease in that ever-frowning face that actually seemed to be a smile. It was there for a moment and then gone.

Peggy, too, seemed to notice a change in her father. She thought it was because she was actually working for once instead of reading one of her books. It had been a long while, probably before Tom's death, that she had seen her father look so tranquil. It eased her worry about him. If he would ever return to his former, more easygoing ways, Peggy thought, then she could concern herself more with Billy, rather than maintaining Father's house and cooking his meals. In a moment of self-righteousness, she thought she never got the credit for the cooking and cleaning and washing she did around the house. That moment, however, was short-lived because of the relief in seeing her father in such good spirits.

"Well, well, Morgan," said Dobbs, "how did you talk Peg into doing your work for you? Or maybe I should ask, why aren't you reading one of her books? Something has gone awry here."

They all laughed. Although the teasing bothered Peggy, mostly because her father was correct, she chuckled out of a gladness to see her father tease again. That was more like things were before the deaths of Tom and her mother.

"Guess who I saw, Peg? Bill. He's in town and I expect he may come by for supper tonight. He had some things to take care of first, though, and won't stop here. He will see us at the house later."

"Well, that means another long night in the kitchen, doesn't it? One night I am going to have you men fix a meal for me, even if I can't stand to eat it."

"Come on, now, it's not that bad," shot back her father. "But don't you worry. I could fix you up a banquet."

"Well, I'd have to see that to believe it," said Peggy. "Seems like I remember a time when Mother was sick and you fixed a meal for Tom and me. I recall we got sicker than Mother."

"That's true, but you got what your mother had. It was nothing to do with my cooking."

"I'm not so sure about that."

"By the way, Morgan," Dobbs intoned, changing the subject, "Bill said he was going to Four Corners tomorrow to bring in another wagon of wood. You plan on going with him. I just don't want to take any chances. What do you say?"

"If you think it's necessary."

"Well, I think so, if I can just keep you from fighting each other. One thing, though, I don't want either of you discussing politics. That'll lead you to a brawl faster than anything I know, considering the mule-headed stubbornness of that Bill."

"That wasn't a nice thing to say about Billy," interjected Peggy.

"May not have been nice, but it was true," answered her father. "He is as stubborn a man as I ever saw, although you may not recognize it since you're pretty stubborn yourself."

"Well," said Peggy in another outbreak of

99

mock outrage, "guess I will just leave and go home, seeing as how I'm so stubborn that if you told me to go and fix supper again, I wouldn't do it."

Peggy took off her apron and reached for her coat. Garrett could have sworn that she looked at the book she had brought with her and then walked out the door, leaving it behind on purpose. Garrett started to call out and remind her, but instead he let her shut the door. The book would give him an excuse to get out tonight since he could return it to her. That way he could see her one more time. If he were going to chop wood with Murphy tomorrow, he doubted he would have a chance to see her then.

After Dobbs left at closing time, Garrett spent more than an hour updating the store's ledgers. If he didn't do that or something else, the time would drag too slowly before he thought it appropriate to return the book. There was a boyish excitement in him that he had not known in years. After what he thought was enough time for Peggy to have finished the meal and the cleaning up, Garrett changed out of his gray clothes and put on the clean ones Peggy had returned. He looked in a mirror and combed his hair as best he could. Finally, he put some more wood in the stove because it was a cold night. He went into the back room to get his gray greatcoat, but as he reached for it, he decided not to wear it, since the uniform sometimes offended Peggy. Despite the cold, he would just go coatless. Picking up *The Merchant of Venice* and sticking it under his arm, he unlocked the door, let himself out and relocked the door.

Once in the street, Garrett was greeted by the cloudless sky and twinkling stars. It was cold now, but it would be even colder by morning. There was a jauntiness in Garrett's step, as he walked away from the store and past the brooding abandoned boarding house across the street. For once, there seemed to be a windless tranquility in Crossrock that was haunted only by the ominous noises of that forsaken building.

It wasn't far to the Dobbs house because had it been, Garrett probably would have turned around to get his coat. He could see his destination and could tell lights were burning in the sitting room and in the kitchen. They might still be eating supper, Garrett thought. Instead of going directly to the front door, he circled behind to catch a glimpse through the kitchen window. If they were still eating, he would come back later.

As Garrett approached, he could see the

table was clean. Then he was shocked to see Peggy in the massive arms of Bill Murphy. Garrett lingered long enough to see Murphy bend down and kiss Peggy on her soft lips. The sight stunned him because it was so unexpected. He started to run back to the store, but he decided to finish his mission. After all, hadn't Peggy left the book at the store, expecting him to return it? Maybe he was mistaken, but it seemed too unlike her ever to forget a book. Garrett's mind raced in the pattern of a man whose feelings have overcome his common sense. He marched up to the front door and banged it hard with his fist. When Dobbs answered, Garrett took the book from under his arm and handed it to him.

"Peggy forgot her book. I thought I would return it in case she wanted to read."

"That's nice of you, Morgan. Come on in, why don't you?"

"I'd better get back to the store," said Garrett. "I didn't think it was this cold outside so I didn't even wear my coat."

Turning from the house, Garrett strode back to the store.

"Don't forget you're to go with Bill tomorrow," Dobbs called from the house.

Garrett didn't answer, pretending not to have heard.

Angry with Peggy and angrier with himself, Garrett stalked back to the store, passing once again the brooding boarding house. Opening the door, then slamming it shut with such force that the bells on the door knob fell to the floor, Garrett locked it behind him and then went straight to his cot for a restless night.

CHAPTER 5

A bitter cold fell over Crossrock during the night. When Garrett awoke the next morning, his mood was only worsened by the weather. His anger turned more on himself than on Peggy. It was probably unjustified for him to have been mad at her in the first place because she had really done nothing intentional. So his anger was directed at himself for letting his feelings add a dimension to his relationship with Peggy that could never work out. Nonetheless, Garrett did not look forward to spending a day with Murphy. Seeing Peggy in Murphy's arms last night had brought to a boil his simmering relationship with Murphy. The smart-aleck's attitude had long grated on Garrett, but he had managed to keep a level head. It was probably more out of respect for old Dobbs than for his daughter that Garrett had not answered back in kind. If pushed any further, though, Garrett realized he might fight back, either with words or with his single fist, regardless of his slim chance against those massive arms of the red-headed Unionist.

Dobbs arrived at the store at his normal time and found Garrett in a surly mood, uncharacteristic of the Alabaman.

"You should have stayed awhile last night," said Dobbs. "Peg said to give you her thanks."

"Don't mention it."

The tone of Garrett's voice told Dobbs something was heavy on the mind of his employee. Perhaps, thought Dobbs, he was worried about the trip with Murphy. No doubt the two, in spite of Garrett's patience with Murphy's impertinence, had trouble getting along. It was unfortunate that they had not taken a liking to each other because they were both good men. Differences in politics and the colored coats which reflected those polarized stands must be too much to overcome for men still in their prime. Dobbs did not guess that his daughter might have been a part of the growing problem.

Garrett was dressed in the gray uniform which he had worn into Crossrock. He could have worn the other outfit given him by Dobbs, but he decided instead on the drab gray uniform, if for no other reason than to antagonize Murphy.

"Bill said he would be by about seven-thirty to pick you up in the wagon."

"You sure he can make it here by then from his place?"

"Oh, no," said Dobbs, "but he stayed the night with us so he could pick you up and get a fairly early start."

"I'm going down to the livery stable to get my horse. I don't relish riding in that wagon with Murphy all day. Anyway, it will be a good chance to give my horse some exercise. I haven't had many like chances the last few weeks."

Garrett picked up his well-worn holster and checked his .44 revolver. It was loaded, as he knew it was. Awkwardly, he strapped on the belt with his one hand by backing up against the doorjamb and holding the belt between his back and the wall so he could fasten the buckle.

"Here," said Dobbs, putting a rifle and scabbard on the adjacent counter. "Take this with you in case you need it. Might come in handy."

"Whatever you say. Is Murphy armed?"

"Yeah, he's got a couple pistols and his shotgun with him."

Putting on the gray coat and his officer's

hat, Garrett picked up the rifle and marched out the door without saying another word.

Quickly, he walked down to the livery stable to get his mount. The street was empty except for the wagon Murphy was driving toward him.

As the two met, Murphy called out, "Aren't you going?"

"I'm going but I'm not riding in that crate with you. I'm gonna give my horse some exercise. Go on and tell Dobbs we're leaving and I will catch up with you just outside town."

The men passed, the gray-coated figure walking on down to the livery stable and the massive figure in the wagon continuing in the opposite direction.

Reaching the stable, he opened one of the double doors and stepped inside into the gloomy interior that smelled of animals. Despite all the holes in the building, they provided little light this time of day and it took Garrett's eyes a moment to adjust.

"Holcomb, you up?"

"Sure, I'm up. The sun's up isn't it? You'll never come in here that you don't find me up," came the reply from behind one of the far stalls.

A moment later a head popped up.

"Oh, it's you, Mr. Garrett. I wasn't sure

who it was and I was afraid it might be Brad Decker. Need your horse?"

"Sure do, how about saddling him up for me," said Garrett, as he walked back to the chestnut's stall. "Say, he's really looking good. Gained back some of that weight, hasn't he."

"Yep, sorta like you. Both of you were a fine sight — skinny as all get-out the day I first saw you. You keep paying me on time and he will gain back even more. Say, this is a pretty cold day just to be doing some riding."

"I'm going out with Bill Murphy to get a wagonload of firewood. Dobbs insists Murphy not go alone out that direction ever since we had that fight with the Decker boys."

"Heard about the fight. Understand you got banged up pretty bad, but that between the two of you you were able to about hold your own until guns were drawn."

"That's true. Of course, I wasn't beat up that bad."

"Hell, as long as you walked away from it you came out the victor. I'd say that was pretty good for a one-armed man," said Holcomb.

Coming from another man, Garrett might have taken offense at Holcomb's remark.

But in dealing with the blacksmith, Garrett had learned Holcomb to be harmlessly outspoken and normally on target with his comments.

"Maybe you are right," said Garrett, "but I don't plan on taking up prize-fighting."

"That Murphy's the one that ought to take up prize-fighting. I've always wondered if when he went out for firewood he didn't just grab a tree with those hams of arms and just pull it up by its roots. When you get back, I want you to tell me if that's so."

"I'll do it, I just hope you believe me when I tell you."

Holcomb finished saddling the horse and handed the reins over to Garrett, who led the animal to the door. He mounted the chestnut for the first time in several weeks. Holcomb opened the door and the rider started through.

"Be careful," Holcomb warned. "That's some rugged territory out there so just watch out."

The warning acknowledged, Garrett gave a kick and sent the chestnut trotting. It felt good to have horseflesh between his legs. Even the cold weather did not detract from that thrill as he paced the horse to catch up with Murphy's wagon.

As Garrett galloped out of Crossrock

109

across the North Fork and toward the horizon, a pair of unfriendly brown eyes watched from a building in town. No doubt about it, Murphy was going to Four Corners for another load of wood and Garrett was going too. Brad Decker might never have noticed had not the horse galloped down the street, the high-spirited pace catching Decker's ear and curiosity. There were a lot of places between Crossrock and Four Corners where a score could be settled and Decker liked that prospect. He would never have bothered had just Murphy been riding out, but with Garrett along Decker could not resist the temptation.

Unsuspecting of those evil eyes staring at him, Garrett was invigorated by the ride. The chestnut, too, was proud to be out of the stable and under Garrett's direction. In no time the horse and rider had caught up with the cumbersome wagon and its brooding driver. The two men who had first encountered each other on the other side of town and not liked each other then, now rode out of Crossrock together as if they were close friends or business partners. They made an unusual contrast — Murphy massive and brooding and Garrett less imposing physically, particularly with the bad left arm, but jaunty at the prospect of getting outdoors on his horse, even if it was with Murphy. One wore a gray army-issue coat and the other wore a blue one that, while not of army derivation, still accurately conveyed by color its wearer's Union sentiments. One said nary a word and the other reveled in talking to his chestnut mount.

During the ride Garrett lost track of time. This was new territory he was riding through and he was amazed at how suddenly the land had changed just two miles out of town. Instead of the level ground that marked the site of Crossrock, the land suddenly dropped, as if they had been riding on a huge plateau. Garrett found himself surveying a rougher more primitive country. This land seemed alien by comparison to what he had previously encountered on his way west from Alabama. While it was apparent Crossrock never got as much rain as it needed, this land looked even thirstier. At least grass did cover the earth and the soil in Crossrock did hold enough promise to sustain a crop, but here the grass was sparser and the other vegetation was the irregularly shaped but hearty desert plants that somehow manage to survive where most other life perishes.

The land looked lifeless. Garrett saw no animals except for a covey of quail huddled under a prickly pear bush for warmth. During warmer weather, Garrett was sure the land would be teeming with rattlesnakes and other varmints, but now it was just unending desolation. It seemed implausible to Garrett that Murphy was leading him through this worthless land in search of wood. Had he and Murphy been on better terms, Garrett might have asked about it, but instead he chose not to bother. Murphy knew what he was doing. It was evident that they were following a wagon trail because Garrett could see the serpentine path weaving between the growing number of small crests and buttes and around the innumerable gullies and ravines. It was strange to be riding through this land that received so little water but was so scarred by the miniscule amount of rainfall it did receive.

Finally, the trail made a turn into what seemed to be the mouth of a small canyon. The further they rode into the canyon the more signs of vegetation Garrett saw. On the canyon walls Garrett noticed meandering trails of ice, the evidence of several natural springs which made the canyon an oasis on an otherwise dreary landscape. About a mile into the canyon, Garrett could see timber. It was not an imposing stand of timber by comparison to his home in Alabama, but it was large by Crossrock standards. The stumps of several trees gave silent testimony that Murphy and perhaps others had come here for wood. In a few minutes they were into the trees, a combination of mesquite and live oaks along with a few other types Garrett did not recognize.

"Here, we are, Garrett. Think you can keep a watch out for me or would you rather handle the ax?"

"Didn't think I came along to chop wood," said Garrett, annoyed by the biting remark aimed at his bad arm. "I'm just here to do the brainwork and keep you out of trouble."

"You didn't do much looking coming out here so I don't know that I can trust you to stand guard. You might fall asleep at your post."

"I won't fall asleep once you start making noise with your ax. Anyway, there was no need to worry on the ride out because no one would have known we were going for wood today unless you told them. No one would have waited all night to shoot at us this early on a cold morning. They'll wait till the sun warms things up a little. The return trip is when we'll have to be on close guard because we'll be slowed down by a full load of firewood, if you ever get started."

Murphy, now the one annoyed by the other's remarks and the logic behind Garrett's reasoning, picked up his ax in disgust and headed to a nearby tree. Soon the ax was in motion and chips of wood flew with each swing. Garrett staked out his chestnut, then unhooked the team and did the same. Taking the rifle from the scabbard on his horse, he walked about a hundred yards down toward the mouth of the canyon. There he found a perch easy enough for him to climb with a rifle in his hand. Sitting down on a rock, he watched the mouth of the canyon, looking for any suspicious signs that they had been followed. He noticed none. Even though the sun was now well overhead, Garrett quickly grew chilled from sitting so he stood up and walked around his small perch for warmth. In a way, he envied Murphy in chopping the wood. The work would keep him warm while Garrett froze on watch. Once, turning around toward Murphy when the chopping had stopped, he saw the massive man building a fire and fetching a coffee pot from the wagon. Now Garrett truly envied Murphy, but he was too prideful to leave his lookout and share Murphy's fire and coffee.

Time passed slowly for Garrett, but even considering that, he was surprised at how quickly Murphy was filling the wagon. In about four hours of solitary work, Murphy had felled three trees, chopped them into manageable size, and loaded the wagon up. Garrett was glad, too, for with a little luck they would make it back to Crossrock before dark.

When he saw Murphy hitching up the team to the wagon, Garrett left his post after a cold, but uneventful stay. Murphy doused the fire with what coffee remained in the blackened pot.

"Get your horse 'cause I'm ready to go," Murphy ordered.

"Go on," said Garrett, "with that load it will take me even less time to catch up with you than it did this morning. Keep your guns handy."

"Hiya," yelled Murphy and the rested team pulled out with authority.

Garrett unstaked his horse, after replacing his rifle in its scabbard. Mounting the chestnut he turned his steed around and began to follow the wagon about fifty yards down the trail. Catching up with the rig, Garrett rode beside Murphy instead of ranging about, as he had done during the morning ride out.

The first three miles were quiet and uneventful, but as they approached the midway point in their return journey, Garrett smelled danger in the air. It was more than just a case of war nerves this time because he thought he saw some movement up ahead where the trail went between two rocky buttes.

"Quick, Murphy, do you see anything up there between those two buttes about a mile ahead?"

"Nothing. Did you see anything?"

"I'm not sure, but that would be a good place for an ambush. Do you think you can get your wagon around that butte to the west instead of following the trail between them?"

"Never tried, but I suppose I can."

"Let's give it a try. This may be all for nothing, but I promised Dobbs I would get you back alive so I don't want to take any chances."

"Look, Garrett, I can take care of myself. You keep forgetting who has the lame arm."

"No I don't Murphy, because you keep reminding me. Now listen. When we get about a quarter mile from the two buttes, cut your wagon off to the west. If there is anybody there, they'll be facing the sun if they come at us. Once you leave the trail ride like the devil because it is going to take you longer to get around than me."

"You planning on running off and leaving me?"

"Yeah, until I get around the butte. If someone is there, they'll probably come around and try to head us off. I want to get there ahead of them and take a position where I can give you some cover."

"Are you sure you actually saw something? I don't want to lose half a load of wood just because you *thought* you saw something."

"You rather risk your firewood or your neck? You just start moving that wagon when I yell."

They rode silently another half mile, nearing the ominous spot on the trail. As Garrett rode, he strained his eyes, trying to see any movement that might verify his suspicions. He saw none. Maybe his imagination was playing tricks on him. Or maybe it was just that four years of war had accustomed him to being careful and not taking unnecessary chances. There were numerous places between Four Corners and Crossrock for an ambush. A hundred ravines along the trail would have served just as well. Why did the two buttes give off such foreboding signals?

"Listen, Murphy, if there's trouble, I will give you all the cover I can. You ride back to Crossrock as fast as the team will take you. It won't be long before dark. If I can get away, I will. If I don't think I can make it in the daylight, I may have to wait until morning to find my way in. Don't come back after me. You got that?"

"Sure, captain," Murphy responded derisively, "any more orders?"

As they got as close to the passage between the buttes as Garrett thought safe, he yelled, "Now!" Spurring his horse he galloped off, keeping as close to the side of the butte as possible to cut down the time it took him to get to the other side.

Half expecting Murphy to ignore his plan, Garrett turned to check if the wagon was following. It was and Murphy was bouncing around like a tumbleweed in a whirlwind, strewing wood as he tried to keep the team on as smooth a course as possible.

Garrett made it to the other side of the butte in good time. Jumping off his horse, he pulled the chestnut to a spot that would provide cover for the animal in case there was trouble. Pulling the rifle from its scabbard, he raced to find a suitable hiding spot for himself. Reaching one that offered adequate cover, he jumped behind the sandstone boulders, taking a last look at Murphy, who was still driving the team at a daring pace. Garrett's breath was heavy, but even his panting did not prevent him from hearing the pounding hooves of approaching horses. Garrett smiled; he had been right. The sound of the horses grew louder until they came around the end of the butte into Garrett's vision. There were three of them — Lucky Ed Skinner and the two Norman brothers — tall with guns drawn and horses set on a course to intersect the wagon.

Garrett leveled the rifle between two abutted rocks and gently squeezed the trigger. The hat of the front-riding Ed Skinner flew into the air and the rider jerked back on the reins of his horse, falling to the ground. If anything, though, Skinner was only grazed because he was on the ground for only an instant before he was scrambling for the cover of a nearby ravine.

The Norman brothers slowed their pace to look at Skinner in disbelief. Two more shots by Garrett persuaded them that it was best to join their companion in the cover of the jagged ravine. Skinner's horse had taken flight with his rifle, but both Normans had had time to get the rifles from their horses. That worried Garrett since the ravine, which he had failed to notice before the shooting started, offered good cover for the trio to maneuver. That meant Garrett would have to be selective about taking additional

119

shots for fear of giving away his location. Another worry was the Normans' horses. Both had stayed relatively close to their riders. It would be easier to escape if he could spook the two remaining horses.

A head peaked up behind a bush at the ravine's edge and Garrett took a hurried shot aimed in haste too great to insure accuracy, but in plenty of time for the head to retreat instinctively. It was probably another hour before darkness which would be Garrett's ally against the three. On the other hand, this was territory that the one-armed man was not familiar with and he needed to get a start soon enough to find the trail back to Crossrock before it was dark. Otherwise, it would be a long, cold night.

Garrett was alone now for Murphy had never stopped, but kept on going to get back the extra time that the Alabaman was buying for him.

A sudden flurry of gunfire kept Garrett low behind his rock wall. Only one of the dozen or so shots hit anywhere near him, telling Garrett that the trio hadn't found his position yet. The gunfire was probably cover for one of the three who was trying to work into position to see Garrett. He eased his eye into an opening among the rocks and stared at the ravine. The Normans' horses were still close enough for his adversaries to reach. It was time to risk a shot to scare the horses away. Otherwise, Garrett was uncertain he could fend them off in a horse-race back to Crossrock. Garrett quickly positioned himself for a shot at the horses. Shooting at the gravel and stones at their feet, he scattered enough gritty projectiles to sting both animals and send them loping off another hundred yards. It wasn't as far as he had hoped, but it would give him time to get to his horse and get a good headstart before any of his enemies could catch a mount.

Now he was worried about his chestnut. The horse was well hidden and accustomed to the sound of gunfire. No doubt the chestnut would be where Garrett left him, but the horse might be shot if he were spotted by the one man Garrett now believed was cautiously crawling over the rocks looking for him. Garrett reloaded his rifle and sent a dozen more shots toward the ravine. He was keeping his revolver in reserve in case things got desperate. It had been thirty minutes since the shooting had begun and it was time for him to work his way back to his horse. Sending one more shot toward the ravine, he ran and jumped into a small gully about halfway between his previous nest and the horse. Waiting a couple minutes, he leaped up and began the final dash for his mount. His hopes for an unseen escape were shattered when three reports of a gun kicked up the ground at his feet. But, never breaking stride, he made it unharmed to his hidden mount.

"Come on, boys, I've got him trapped!" yelled his invisible assailant.

Now the tables had turned and Garrett was the one being attacked from an unseen position. Waiting for the other two to take a position over him was certain death, so Garrett shoved his rifle back into the scabbard and climbed awkwardly into the saddle. Leaning down around the horse's neck, he kicked the chestnut in the flank and dashed out into the open. Apparently surprised at the sudden and mounted appearance of Garrett, the gunman above the rider did not get off a quick shot. The extra seconds gave Garrett time to get out of easy range. Still, four shots too close for comfort told Garrett he had a way to go before he was in the clear.

"Go get the horses," shouted that still unseen gunman. "He's making a run for Crossrock."

Garrett by then was too far away to hear the shout over the noise of his streaking horse, but he rode the chestnut like he knew he was being tailed. His horse was still a good one, he could tell by the strength with which the animal maneuvered in the dusk. He had to pick up the trail to Crossrock and finding it would take him closer to, rather than away from, his three attackers. Looking back to his right about three-quarters of a mile, he could see two riders coming his way. When Garrett turned back to check the direction he was taking, the chestnut leaped a ten-foot-wide gully which had suddenly appeared beneath the mount and rider. The startled horse jumped awkwardly to make the other side and did so successfully, but the unprepared Garrett was slung forward, his head striking that of the horse. The sudden, hard blow had caught Garrett unexpectedly and he was dizzy momentarily. He could feel the blood streaming from his nose and down his face onto his clothes. The taste of the blood, though, snapped Garrett out of his brief dizziness and he implored his mount on. About a mile farther he recognized the landmarks and realized he was back on the trail again. However, the riders were closing on him and he could hear gunshots. It was foolish even to try to return the fire. With his lame arm bouncing with every jolting step, Garrett could not afford a shot for fear of losing his balance. That meant a more certain fate than trying to outrun the bullets.

The skies had turned darker and Garrett looked vainly for the twinkling lights that would tell him he was nearing Crossrock. He knew the chestnut was tiring, so he eased up a little on the mount, since the growing darkness would once again contribute to his advantage now that he had found the trail. His horse, though, sensed the danger and kept up the pace until they came into sight of the lights of Crossrock. Both man and mount sensed relief. Garrett doubted that the two riders on his tail would follow him all the way into town. Nonetheless, he was uncertain if Decker and the man they called Snuff might not be waiting for him just outside town. Taking no chances, he left the trail and circled around Crossrock, coming in from the opposite direction. Dismounting when he reached the first building, Garrett pulled his revolver from its holster and carried it at his side for quick use. The chestnut followed him as he quietly made his way to the back door of the livery stable. Pausing a moment at the door, he heard an alien voice, not Holcomb's rasping. Garrett was uncertain whose voice it was, but he knew it was up to no good.

Silently, Garrett opened the door a crack. Inside he could see Holcomb being shoved up against the wall of the nearest stall. It was the man Murphy had called Snuff, one of Decker's allies.

"If Lefty gets back, old man, you had better come and tell me or I'll give you a beating like you've never had before," said Snuff.

"This is what I think of your threats," said Holcomb, who spit in the ruffian's face.

Instantly, Snuff took his pistol from his holster and smashed it up against the face of the blacksmith.

Garrett, surprised that Holcomb was still standing, quietly slipped in the door. As Snuff prepared to hit the blacksmith again, Garrett used his own pistol as a club and sent a crashing blow to the bearded man's head. Snuff fell instantly to the ground.

"You okay?"

"Better than I would have been if you hadn't shown up. I owe you one. Say, you're sorta bloody yourself, did they get you?"

"No, my horse and I bumped heads on the way back. If you owe me one, then get me a bucket of water."

Holcomb obliged while Garrett picked up Snuff's sidearm.

"Dump it on him," instructed Garrett

125

when Holcomb returned.

The unconscious man came to with Garrett standing over his face.

"I'm here," said Garrett, "so you go tell that to your friend Decker and tell those three you sent out to bushwhack me that they missed. Now get out of here."

The ruffian scurried out of the stable into the street.

"My mount is out back. Would you bring him in and take care of him? He's had a hard day."

"Sure will. I'll do it for free even."

"No, I'll settle with you later, but I want to get back to the store to see if Murphy made it back okay."

"I guess he did, I saw him ride into town like he was running from the devil. Did they try to ambush you?"

"Yeah, just like everyone expected," said Garrett. "I'll tell you about it later. I need to get to the store."

Cautiously, Garrett left the stable by the back and worked his way down the street to the store. He was tired, aching all over, and the blood that covered his face was dried and cracked. His coat was stained black with blood all down the front.

Approaching the store from the rear, he could hear someone inside in his room.

Stealthily, he worked his way to the front door, revolver in hand. At the door, he turned the knob. Ominously, the door was unlocked. With the gun in his hand, he clumsily opened the door, hoping to slip in on who was in the back room. But, he had forgotten about the bells on the knob and their ringing brought a figure from out of the back room. He raised his gun to shoot.

"Oh, my God," said Peggy Dobbs, startled by the blood all over Garrett's face and clothes. "They got you too."

"No, I'm fine," said Garrett, after holstering his pistol. "How bad is Murphy?"

"It's not him," sobbed Peggy. "They got Father. He's beat up pretty bad."

CHAPTER 6

A fortnight of serenity in Crossrock followed the fateful day when Garrett and Murphy went for wood. For Dobbs it was a time of recuperation from the beating he had received that night. The old man seemed to be recovering better physically than emotionally. Although he had been robbed of two day's receipts totaling eleven dollars, that was of minor concern to Dobbs. The loss of the pocket watch — Tom's watch with the bent cover — disturbed Dobbs greatly. One day when she had stopped by the store, Peggy told Garrett her father seemed to be more distraught over losing the watch than she remembered him being when word of Tom's death reached him. Then, he had seemed so calm that he was a pillar of strength for Peggy and her mother. Now the pain of the beating was not nearly as great as the agony from the missing watch.

While Peggy stayed home days to nurse her father back to health, Garrett ran the store almost alone. He stayed busy, but it was not an impossible chore, even for a one-armed man. In the last two weeks he had seen little of Peggy except when she stopped by the store, either to bring him lunch or to fetch something needed at home. Garrett enjoyed her unexpected visits. Many days about noon she would bring him a hot meal. Those were the days Garrett enjoyed most because she would stay long enough for him to eat so she could take back the dishes. It gave him a break and a chance to talk with the beautiful young woman. On days she did not come in with a meal before noon, Garrett would lock up the store for thirty minutes and go over to the Benton Saloon for a disappointing meal. On those days, however, Peggy would always drop by later in the afternoon to check up on things at the store for her father. That was the only good thing about Peggy not bringing him his lunch; he at least had something to look forward to in the afternoon.

If Garrett had seen little of Peggy, he had seen even less of Murphy since they escaped the ambush. That night Garrett had found Murphy and Peggy with the bruised Dobbs in the back room of the store, the old man sprawled out on Garrett's cot. The old man was beaten about the head pretty badly and was unconscious when Garrett first saw him. Later, Peggy filled Garrett in on what had happened. When Murphy reached Crossrock with his load of wood, he went straight to the Dobbs house where he told the old man and Peggy what had happened. Then asking Dobbs for the use of his horse, Murphy went out back to saddle it up to ride back for Garrett. Dobbs, who was worried about Garrett, decided to walk to the store to wait for the Alabaman. After her father left, Peggy grew scared, but caught Murphy before he rode away and persuaded him to carry her to the store where she could wait with her father. But as their horse approached the store, it seemed to shy away from something on the ground. There, in the street in front of the store, they found the unconscious Dobbs.

Thinking first her father was dead, Peggy shrieked, but a soft moaning from the crumpled figure in the dusty street calmed her. She unlocked the door as Murphy carried the old man into the back room. Peggy had lost track of time as she worried over her father and forgot her worries about Garrett. Only when she heard the jangling of the door bell and stepped into the front room to find Garrett pointing his revolver at her did she remember the Alabaman's plight.

With Garrett's assistance, Murphy carried the dazed Dobbs back home. Garrett's drawn revolver provided a bit of unneeded protection for them. As they carried the old man, Garrett sensed the fear that night in Peggy's voice. Although every fiber in his body was against it, Garrett actually suggested that Murphy stay the night in the Dobbs house, just in case there was more trouble. Murphy agreed and he had spent every night since in the front room of the house. Garrett envied Murphy for his time with Peggy, but he felt better knowing she was protected. Except for two occasions when he had seen the massive man walking down the street, Garrett had not glimpsed, much less talked to Murphy since that night. Garrett wasn't sure why Murphy had not stopped by to talk about the trip to Four Corners and to discuss what precautions they would need to take to protect themselves from the Decker boys in the future. He suspected, however, that Murphy did not want to admit that Garrett's sharp eyes had probably saved both of their lives.

Five men Garrett had seen nothing of in the two weeks since the attempted ambush were Brad Decker and his cohorts. Their absence, more than anything else, was responsible for the calm which seemed to be re-establishing itself in Crossrock and in the lives of Garrett, Dobbs, Peggy and Murphy. However, that tranquility would be shattered the first time he ran into any of the Decker bunch, Garrett vowed.

It was a warm morning, one of those unpredictably pretty days that periodically spring up in Texas winters, when old man Dobbs returned to the store. It had been seventeen days since Dobbs had been there, so his mid-morning appearance surprised Garrett. The Alabaman, in one of those few brief moments of idleness since he had taken to running things alone, was seated behind the counter, taking a breather.

"I see you're working quite hard," Dobbs laughed.

"Well, good morning! How are you feeling these days?"

"Better, much better. But I lost my watch, Tom's watch. Did Peg tell you the watch was stolen?"

"That's what I heard."

"Wish now I had just given it to you. At least then I'd know it was in decent hands."

"Any idea who did it? Was it Decker or one of his friends?"

"I'm not sure," said Dobbs, his brow furrowed. "I never saw anyone. Whoever it was must have been waiting beside the building and then slipped behind me as I passed. You know my watch was stolen, don't you?"

"Yeah," answered Garrett, who pitied the old man for his obsession with the lost watch.

"Did I tell you that Decker and I had words that day?"

"No," said Garrett, "nobody did, not even Peggy."

"Well, I haven't told anyone 'til now. Peggy was out of the store when Decker came in and at the time I didn't think it would do anything but scare her, if I told her."

"Tell me what happened."

"The store was empty when he came in late in the afternoon. He wanted me to let you go. Said you was a troublemaker that would do nothing but bring harm to me and my family. When I told him I wouldn't do it, he just said he had given fair warning and hoped nobody close to me got hurt."

"Anything else said?"

"Nope, that was it. I didn't really think much about it then, but it's sure made me think he or his boys were the ones that beat me up. Say, you don't reckon that watch could have fallen out of my pocket in the street do you?"

"I doubt it," said Garrett.

"I'll tell you what," said Dobbs looking outside the store window, "you've shown you can handle this store alone, so I'm going to leave you to it. I'll start tomorrow to come in a little in the morning and in the afternoon or I'll send Peggy to do so and relieve you a little. I need to go now."

Garrett watched as Dobbs, walking with a stoop he hadn't noticed before, left the store. Once out in the street, Dobbs threw himself down on his hands and knees and began crawling around in front of the store, sifting the dust between his fingers. After ten minutes of this, the old man stood up and slowly headed home. Garrett's pity for the old man was deep, but he didn't know what he could do to ease Dobb's mind about the watch.

When Peggy did not bring lunch before noon that day, he closed up the store and hurried over to the Benton Saloon for his meal. When he returned, he found the store unlocked and Peggy waiting on a customer.

"Sorry I was late," she greeted him as he came in the door. "I brought you a lunch, if you're still hungry."

"I'll save it for supper," said Garrett.

"Anyway, what are you doing here? I didn't expect you 'til later."

"Just a minute," she said, taking some coins from the old woman she had been waiting on.

Garrett went to the back to get his apron as the old woman left.

"Father's better now, at least better in some ways, than he has been so I thought I would come down and help out. I know you've been busy."

"It hasn't been that bad."

"Maybe not, but we couldn't have made it these past few weeks without you. Come here and let me tie that apron for you."

Garrett obeyed her so he could enjoy her touch. Then she turned him around and took his right wrist with its unbuttoned cuff and pulled him toward her. Peggy surprised Garrett with a gentle kiss on the cheek.

"That's just for being such a big help. Father and I both appreciate it."

Garrett was stunned. It had only been a sisterly kiss, unlike the one he had seen her exchanging with Murphy that night through the kitchen window, but it was a welcomed surprise.

"Can I ask you something?" inquired Peggy after a pause.

"Sure, but I've always been suspicious of

135

girls who kiss you and then have something to ask you."

"It's nothing like that," she shot back, "I've just noticed that lots of times your right cuff is unbuttoned. I mean that is your good hand. Why don't you button it?"

"Have you ever tried to button your right cuff with your right hand? Well, I have and you can't do it. It takes a left hand. It may seem like it should be buttoned, but without a good left hand I can't do it."

"I'm sorry," she stammered, "that was thoughtless of me, but it just looked . . . I mean I had noticed it undone . . . and, oh, I don't know."

"No harm done. There are just a lot of things I have learned you take for granted with two hands. I can unbutton my cuff with my teeth, but I sure can't button it up. Funny, isn't it?"

"I'll fix that," she said, once more reaching for his right wrist. "Let me button it for you."

Taking his hand in hers, she buttoned the cuff and gave his hand a little squeeze that told Garrett she was sorry for her thoughtlessness.

"I'd better be going now because I ought to check on Father. He plans to start coming in some each day, starting tomorrow, so

136

be prepared. Whatever you do, please don't bring up that watch. I wish now you'd forgotten to give it back to him. The loss is driving him crazy."

"I won't mention it."

Peggy turned and left the store. Garrett was befuddled by her sudden tenderness toward him. It was a moment that he had longed for, yet never expected to enjoy because of her feeling for Murphy. Garrett took a perverse pleasure in wondering what Murphy would have done had he witnessed that kiss. The idea was enough for Garrett to forget the time the roles were reversed and he had seen Murphy kissing her. But then he realized all this probably meant nothing. Nonetheless, Garrett had enjoyed the sweet smell of Peggy's hair, the warmth of her breath and the tenderness of her lips as she kissed him. He still had that for a memory, regardless of Peggy's motive.

A week after Peggy planted the kiss on Garrett's cheek, Murphy came by the store at mid-morning to tell Garrett she would not be able to bring him lunch that day. Her father was feeling unusually weak and she would stay the day with him, Murphy said. Then turning to leave, he took a few tentative steps toward the door. Stopping, he spun around to face Garrett.

"You've been a big help to us," said the huge man. "We would have had a rougher time without you and I just want you to know I appreciate it. I knew this before now, but I'm a stubborn cuss and the color of your clothes kept me from admitting it to you. Thanks."

Then Murphy, who had never wondered if all the trouble might have been avoided by Dobbs not hiring Garrett, extended his hand. Garrett grabbed it. It was a firm handshake and with it the two men, who on the field of war would have been enemies and who had become suspicious allies only because of the trouble in Crossrock, put those difficulties behind them.

"I don't know if anyone told you," continued Murphy, "but I was coming back after you the night we were ambushed."

"Peggy told me," said Garrett. "She explained it all."

"I didn't desert you. I just thought I had better try to get her father taken care of."

"I know you didn't run out on me. Anyway, I told you not to return for me. I might have shot you, thinking you were one of them."

Unburdened of that load of conscience, Murphy departed the store, leaving Garrett to his thoughts. That was a slow morning with only two other folks coming in to make purchases. Even the old men who had always gathered around the stove to talk politics with Dobbs had seldom dropped by for very long in the days following the storekeeper's beating. Instead of seeking busywork, as was his usual custom on slow days, Garrett just took a seat on the stool behind the counter, watching out the window and pondering when he ought to leave Crossrock.

Had he been busy, Garrett might never have seen Decker and his boys as they rode by the store. It was the first time he had seen any of them since the night of the ambush and Dobbs's beating. The anger welled up in him as they passed and he had to fight the urge to go outside after them. Maybe the five were just riding through. If not, Garrett knew there would be trouble. The slow rage seemed almost to consume him. When he finally snapped out of that angry stupor, it was five minutes after noon and past time for him to run down to the Benton Saloon for a quick lunch, since Peggy had sent word by Murphy that she was not bringing food.

Thinking of Decker reminded Garrett of Dobbs's admonition to wear his sidearm whenever he left the store. Going into his room, Garrett pulled his revolver from its holster. It had a full load. Then he reholstered the gun and awkwardly managed to buckle it on with his one hand and the help of the door frame he had backed up against. Going out of the front door, he looked down the street. There in front of the saloon, he saw five hitched horses. The excitement welled up inside him, as he turned to lock the door behind him. A wise man might have opted to go without lunch that day, but the sight of the mounts only increased Garrett's hunger, either for food or for a showdown. He knew not which. His strides seemed to grow in length the closer he got to the saloon. By the time he reached the mounts, Garrett was almost at a trot. It was an exhilaration, a foolish one perhaps, like he had once felt when riding into a sure battle during the war. He paused a moment outside the door and listened to the loud talking and the horseplay from the five men. Then, clearing his throat, Garrett strode inside the saloon with the confidence that comes from a belief in one's cause. He fairly slammed the door, startling the Decker boys and leaving Benton and his wife, Maude, with their mouths agape.

"Come in, Mr. Garrett," said Benton. "Want a plate for lunch?"

"Sure," said Garrett, eyeing the back table where the five men were seated, "that's what I came for."

Startled at seeing Garrett so boldly entering their domain, the Decker boys were strangely silent, unlike the jabbering and laughing Garrett had heard outside the door. Then, all at once realizing Garrett was badly outnumbered, the five men began to chuckle sinisterly.

"Hello, Lefty," said Decker. "Haven't seen you in a few days."

"I've been in town where I always am. Where've you been lately? Looking for some more old men to beat up?"

"Yeah, I heard about Dobbs getting robbed and beat, but I don't know anything about that. It's a shame, but we don't go in for attacking old men."

"That's a lie and you know it because I saw your buddy Snuff there pistol-whip Holcomb down at the livery stable. He might have killed Holcomb had I not outrun your other three assassins that night. What were you doing while this was going on?"

"Calling someone a liar's pretty strong words," said Decker, restraining Snuff from getting up from the table.

"Real strong words when they're true," Garrett retorted.

Decker stood up from his table and his four companions quickly pushed their chairs back and moved to the side of the room.

"All right, boys," shouted Benton, leveling toward Decker the shotgun that he kept behind the counter. "I don't want any gunplay in here. Move it out in the streets."

"I'm with you," Decker huffed, "I don't want to kill Lefty with my gun. I want to do it with my hands."

Unbuckling his gunbelt, Decker let his pistol fall to the floor.

"You too yellow to go at it with fists, Lefty?"

"It's not a fair fight, Brad, and you know it," said Benton, nervously. "He's only got one arm."

"I'm just going to use one arm," said Decker, sneering. "Snuff, you and Ed find something to tie my left arm down with. Lefty, you gonna fight or not? If so, take off your gunbelt. If not, get out of my sight and don't ever let me see you again in Crossrock."

"I'll fight," said Garrett, "but first have all your friends put their guns on the counter where Benton can keep them. I'm not going to be shot in the back by one of your henchmen when I'm through with you."

"Do what he says, boys. This won't take

142

long. In fact," said Decker, taking a watch from his britches pocket, "I'll be through with him in five minutes."

As Decker's men put their sidearms on the counter, Garrett unbuckled his gunbelt and gave it to Maude.

"Go get Murphy," he whispered to Maude. "He's at Dobbs's house. I may need him to keep this a fair fight."

"Yes, sir," Decker continued, as he looked at the watch, "we'll be back in here finishing our meal by twelve-twenty and Garrett will have to crawl out or be carried out."

Garrett eyed Decker sternly, ignoring the bravado, until his glance caught the gleam of the watch with the familiar embossed case. Garrett stared even harder at the watch. Sure enough, the cover was embossed with a dented "D."

"Where'd you get that watch?" challenged Garrett. "You take it when you beat up Dobbs?"

"My pap gave me this watch many years ago," lied Decker, as he put it back in his britches pocket.

"Now I know you're a liar."

Snuff broke up the argument as he began to tie a length of cord he had found around Decker's left arm. Then he looped the cord around Decker's waist, cinching it and making the left arm immobile.

"Okay, Lefty, we're even. My right arm against your right arm."

"Hold it," interrupted the nervous Benton again. "You boys settle this outside. I don't want my place torn up, you understand?"

Outside the men marched, Decker leading the way, followed by his four companions, Garrett and then Benton, who shut the door and stood guard over his saloon with his shotgun cradled in his left arm. Into the street the two combatants marched until Decker turned around. Face to face they began to stalk one another. Silently, the two men trailed each other in a circle, neither coming within striking distance. Their awkward maneuvers were stark evidence of the limits of one-armed combat. Decker, unused to the bound arm, almost stumbled to the ground in his first feint at Garrett. Garrett's mobility was better, but certainly not the match for an unbound, two-armed man.

After circling each other several times it was Decker who landed the first blow in a rush at Garrett and made him all the madder. Garrett's retaliatory swing missed its mark to the shouts of Decker's companions. Gaining confidence from his hit and Garrett's miss, Decker moved in for another blow. Garrett, however, anticipating this one, ducked out of its path and landed a solid fist in Decker's stomach.

Surprised at his miss and Garrett's well-aimed counter-punch to his stomach, Decker backed up, then charged again. This time he flailed away with his arm, striking Garrett on the jaw and shoulder. Garrett, too, was swinging wildly at his opponent in close proximity. Several of his blows also hit target, but they were not the solid punches Garrett was seeking. Backing off from one another, the two enemies caught their breath and then both, as if of the same mind, charged each other. They fell to the ground, rolling over and over in the dust of the street. By this time a crowd had gathered, most silently pulling for Garrett, but intimidated by the noisy presence of Decker's four henchmen.

When the rolling on the ground stopped, Decker was on top, slamming Garrett's face with bloody accuracy. Garrett, though, managed to lift his body up to unbalance Decker, who fell back just enough for Garrett to wrap his leg over Decker's head and lay him back on the ground.

Both men hustled back to their feet, each spitting dust from his mouth. Decker's face was puffy but not bloodied. Garrett's nose

145

was bleeding profusely. Undeterred though, Garrett waded back into Decker with a blow which knocked the ringleader off balance. But as Garrett moved in to strike, Decker pulled his legs from under him and they were both on the ground again. Rolling around once more they alternately struck each other and the ground with their misses. This time Garrett stopped on top and began to pummel Decker's face with a barrage of savage blows.

In desperation, Decker reached for Garrett's throat but was unable to grasp it. Grabbing a handful of sand, Decker threw it into Garrett's eyes. The stinging pain broke Garrett's windmill of punches long enough for Decker to knock the Alabaman off and stand up. With Garrett on his knees, still rubbing his eyes in an effort to see, Decker rushed up and kicked him in the ribs. Garrett fell down, rolling over on his back. Decker, aiming his right foot for Garrett's throat, kicked again, but the blinded Garrett somehow managed to move in time to avoid the blow and to grab Decker's other leg. Decker then fell to the ground with a force all the more stunning because of its unexpectedness. Garrett then clambered on top of the downed Decker. With his eyes shut and aching and blood running down his face and clothes, Garrett did not even try to strike Decker. Instead, he just grabbed the still stunned man by the throat and began to squeeze with all his might. Decker's strength was waning, Garrett could feel as he put all his will into killing his opponent. Garrett could tell from the slowed breathing and the gurgling noises that Decker was under his control.

"Stay back, boys," Garrett heard Benton say, "because I've got a shotgun here that will kill the first man that interferes. Do you hear that, Snuff?"

"You heard him," Garrett heard another voice say. "I've got a shotgun here, too, that says they can finish the fight up."

Never before had Garrett been so grateful to hear Murphy's voice. Garrett, who still could not see, realized he had won the fight, if Decker's companions were considering breaking it up. The struggle from Decker was now over. The man was motionless. Garrett did not think he was dead, but he was not sure. Standing up over the stilled figure, Garrett tried to wipe the grit, stinging sweat and blood from his eyes. After regaining blurred vision, Garrett stepped back, cocked his foot and kicked Decker in the ribs, returning the hardcase's earlier favor.

147

"That's for the one you got in on me," said Garrett.

Then, bending over the prone figure, Garrett stuck his hand in Decker's britches pocket and retrieved the watch. Shielding it from prying eyes with his hand, Garrett put it in his own pocket.

"Get my gun for me, would you, Mr. Benton?" asked Garrett, his energy and strength sapped. "I've got to get back to work."

"No, you're not," Peggy Dobbs said, grasping his arm. "We'll close the store down so you can get cleaned up and get some rest. You just hold onto my arm and I'll help you back to the store. Billy will follow us with his shotgun to make sure nobody tries to take a shot at you."

Garrett, still half-blinded, stumbled back to the store, trying not to pass out. Once inside, Peggy helped him to his cot while Murphy relocked the door.

"That was brave of you," said Peggy to Garrett, who was oblivious to everything but the pain in his body.

Murphy just stood over Garrett, shaking his head at the bloodied body and face of the Alabaman.

"Garrett," he said, "I just wish for once

148

you would get in a fight you didn't come out of looking like the loser."

CHAPTER 7

At no time in the last three years had Peggy Dobbs felt safer walking the streets of Crossrock than in the aftermath of Garrett's triumph over Decker. That sinister Decker, with the facial scars that whispered of some calamity like the murder of Mrs. Dawson and her two daughters, had long frightened Peggy. Decker's aloofness to Peggy, the most desirable woman in Crossrock, worried her to an otherwise unmerited cautiousness. Peggy even saw the irony of events which left her at ease in going about Crossrock. The massive Murphy with those huge, powerful arms had never been able to erase that deep-seated fear Peggy harbored for Decker. Yet here was the crippled Garrett, a man with only one good arm, who had outfought Decker and continued to show no fear of the fellow and his four ruffians. It was like something out of Shakespeare or the mythology she enjoyed.

Peggy's gratitude over the removal of that fearful burden manifested itself in a growing warmth for Garrett, maybe even an affection for the former Confederate officer. This Peggy would never admit to herself, but Garrett noticed a more cordial response from her than he had ever expected possible. Peggy still buttoned the cuff on Garrett's right sleeve every day when she first came to the store. It was a simple, but meaningful gesture of her acceptance of him. Neither Garrett nor Peggy took it for much more than a friendly gesture or courtesy, but still there was something special for the Alabaman the moment their hands touched in that daily ritual.

Garrett had impressed Peggy with his solid working habits and the pleasure he took in his work. From working with him, she had learned that Garrett had the manners and education of a Southern gentleman, but she knew little more than that about his background. She never asked him about his past because her father had taught her it was impolite to be too inquisitive. Instead, she watched him more openly as he went about his chores and her imagination filled in the missing details of his life. It was often funny when Garrett tried to do a chore which required two hands, like sweeping. Peggy had to stifle her small laughs, not so much at his awkwardness, but at his ingenuity in overcoming the situation with his one hand.

While these moments with him added greatly to her affection for Garrett, one incident made her almost sisterly in her devotion to him. Two days after the fight with Decker, Garrett, who was still badly bruised from the encounter, told Dobbs he had something for him. Reaching into his pocket, Garrett had pulled out Tom's watch.

Peggy cried as she watched her father, shaking all over, reach out and take the watch from Garrett. Tears welled in the man's eyes and he stood there speechless as he caressed the watch with a tenderness that left no doubt about his love for his lost son.

"I found it on Decker," said Garrett. "You've been so good to me that the least I could do was return the watch to you."

"Thank you, thank you a lot," the emotional Dobbs was finally able to say.

Peggy ran to Garrett and wrapped her arms around him in a warm embrace topped off with a kiss on his cheek.

"Oh, thank you. You just don't know how much this means to me and Father. I just don't know what we would have done without you these last few weeks."

"You'd have made it," said Garrett. "If it hadn't been for me this probably never would have happened anyway."

"You just forget that thought," Peggy shot back. "Something was bound to give around here eventually with Brad Decker. With you here at least one man will stand up to them."

As she talked, her father put on his coat and walked out the door without saying another word. Peggy turned to follow, but decided against it. Father probably would not want her to see him cry, she thought, and that was what he was doing. Not since the watch was stolen had she seen him this emotional. As her father shut the door and walked out into the street, for the first time in her life Peggy saw him as an old man, not the strong vigorous father she had previously known.

"Father looks much older than I've ever realized before," she told Garrett. "I guess the death of Tom and Mother and then the disappearance of the watch took more out of him than I had thought possible. I know you want to leave in the spring, but would you consider staying to run the store for him?"

Garrett was stunned for he had never given any thought to staying. Although Peggy was good inducement for living in

Crossrock awhile longer, Garrett hated the idea of seeing her marry Murphy, as he figured she ultimately would. Still, Crossrock would provide a job for him and that was more of a certainty than what might be ahead for him out west.

"Don't answer right now. Just think about it," said Peggy, sensing his uncertainty and fearing a negative response. "I don't know how much longer Father is going to be able to handle things. Please think about staying."

"I'll give it some thought, but that doesn't mean I am going to stay. You've got to remember that."

"I will," she said, "but you remember that I want you to stay for Father and for me. It's getting about time for me to fix his supper, but I will see you in the morning and we can talk more then."

Garrett watched as she put on her coat and left the store, leaving him puzzling over her comments and her sudden desire for him to stay. He was sure she had not consulted her father, nor Murphy, about her request. She was surely just thinking about her father's well-being, thought Garrett, but maybe there was a chance she wanted him to stay near her. His mind was awash in a sea of conflicts. While he did not like Crossrock and the surrounding country, Peggy's presence more than compensated for that. Further, he did not envision himself spending the rest of his life as a storekeeper. There were just too many opportunities in the new country for success and riches. A man with his background and education might, with a few breaks, be able to make a fortune. The lame arm was certainly a liability, but Garrett always put more stock in his brain than his brawn. The necessity of stopping his western journey for the winter had now given him several decisions he had never realized he would have to make. A choice would have been easy except for one thing — Peggy.

Images of her gentle beauty kept coming to Garrett's mind, as if she were imploring him to stay. Her soft brown hair, those pretty blue eyes, her tender skin, her gentle touch all haunted his thoughts and blocked his normal decisiveness honed by months of leading men through war. Remembering her soft kisses troubled him, too. Oh, how he wanted to embrace her tightly and press his lips to hers so she would know how he really felt about her, but that would have been a dangerous course because he was never sure of her feelings for him. Sure, she had kissed him, asked him to stay, but it could well be out of little more than friendship. If that were the case, it would be the cruelest blow of all to Garrett. Just a smattering of affection or even total rejection from a desired woman is easier for a man to accept than simple friendship. That is the most vicious of love's unpredictable verdicts and what scared Garrett most. It was the reason he was inclined to go ahead with his plans to move on in the spring. There were just too many obstacles between him and Peggy. He had been married before while she was still virginal. His background and hers were complete opposites. He was trying to escape an unpleasant past; she was building her future. Finally, there was Murphy, a man Garrett knew would accept the loss of Peggy with little grace. There were just too many problems.

By the next morning, Garrett had made up his mind to stick with his plans to leave in the spring. He was resolved to tell Peggy at his first opportunity just to be done with it. He did not care to prolong a decision that would ultimately lead to her disappointment. But when the ringing of the bells on the door heralded her appearance the next day, he didn't even get a chance to bring it up. Peggy did, beginning where she had left off the afternoon before.

"Father's not coming in today," she said. "He's not really feeling well. This is what I mean when I tell you we are going to need some help in keeping things running around here. Have you had a chance to think about my request?"

All night he had thought about his decision and how he would tell Peggy, but those plans were useless now. He was on the defensive. And yet, even though his mind thought it best to say no, his courage deserted him. He couldn't.

"Thought, yes," said Garrett. "I've thought about little else since last night. Decision, no. It's not like spring weather gets here next week. There's still going to be a lot of cold weather and I don't plan on leaving before that's over."

"That's not very reassuring," Peggy stated, as she ran her hand through her long brown hair.

"I wish I could be, but I can't right now. It's just that I didn't see Crossrock as a permanent stopover when I arrived and the thought still troubles me. Sure, I'm indebted to your father because he has treated me well as a person and a hand, particularly considering that I fought for the South. But I have tried to repay that debt with a fair day's work and a helping hand in dealing

157

with Decker's bunch."

"Well, what do you think Decker will do when you leave?"

"I can't say, but if he operates like he has in the past, he'll probably bushwhack me."

"It's not just you, though. What about me? Or Father? Do you think they'll leave us alone?"

"Look, law and order is going to catch up with them. Sure, it may be bad now, but remember it was just seven or so months ago that Lee surrendered. This is defeated country and it will take time to reestablish the normal lawful order."

"But will that be too late for us?"

"Peggy, I can't say, but you've got Murphy to look out for you and he's a whole man with two good arms. He can take care of himself and you and your father."

"Billy doesn't work in the store and when he's busy on his place there is no one in town who would stand up for Father and me. I don't feel safe without you around."

"Well, I'm sure Murphy would love to have me hanging around after you two get married. If that's the plan, then I'm not part of it and I can give you your answer now, but you won't like it."

"That's not what I meant," she replied with a hurt look in her eyes that made

Garrett sorry about his statement. "I don't know what my plans are and I'm not even sure what Billy's plans are either. I've thought he would have wanted to get married by now, but he's too busy trying to get his land in working shape to bother."

Garrett could not believe what he had just heard. Perhaps Peggy's growing friendship did have a basis in affection, maybe even love. Then again, maybe she was a little shrewder than he thought; maybe she was using this uncertainty about her future as a pretext for getting him to stay longer in Crossrock.

"That's between you and Murphy. Don't get me involved in this business because Murphy's suspicious of me around you anyway."

"Should he be?"

"Probably," Garrett said before he realized the turn the conversation had taken and the significance of his answer. That one word tip-off was the first time he had even remotely made his feelings known to Peggy.

"I thought so," she responded in an answer that left Garrett even more surprised.

With that, Peggy walked over and grasped Garrett by his good hand. Looking deeply into his eyes, she buttoned his cuff and said nothing more.

They worked in silence for thirty minutes. Garrett's quietness was more one of disbelief at what had been said and at the possibility that she shared some of his feelings than one of intent. Peggy did not speak out of a beguiling feminine coyness. It had taken her a long time to admit it to herself, but there was something about Garrett that was appealing. Certainly, he had shown himself adept at running the store, she thought. The merchant's life was one she had grown accustomed to and Peggy now questioned whether or not she could adapt to the rigors of the farm life Murphy had planned for her after marriage. If she could just persuade Garrett to stay, then she would have time to make a final decision between the two men who now played such a large part in her life. Finally, Peggy broke the silence.

"Could I ask you some questions?"

"Sure," said Garrett not knowing what to expect, but relieved that the long silence was ending. "Go ahead. What do you want to know?"

"Oh, just some things about you."

"There's not really much to know. I'm from Mallory County, Alabama, and I'm heading west — if you aren't successful in convincing me I've gone far enough."

"Why? Why didn't you stay in Alabama

160

after the war?"

"There were just too many unpleasant memories. That's all. I guess I figured I could make a new start better without having to rebuild my past."

"What memories?"

"I lost my wife and two boys," Garrett told Peggy, who had anticipated the wife but not the children. "That was too great a loss to live with, but I guess you understand that because of Tom and your mother."

"Did soldiers kill them?"

"No, I suppose I would really have been bitter had that happened, but it was cholera that killed them. They were buried on my place, or what was my place, when I got back from the war."

"I'm sorry," said Peggy. "I didn't mean to bring back unpleasant memories."

"I don't guess they're bad memories because they made a fine family, but losing them hurt. There was just no way to get over it by staying there. Too many reminders."

"What kind of place did you have?"

"It was a farm of about two-hundred acres. We grew a lot of cotton."

"You owned slaves, I guess?"

"Some. Most of my neighbors did too."

"Did it ever bother you? I mean Father always said it was wrong and mean to own

161

someone else."

"It never bothered me because it was a way of life I grew up with. Now you tell me something! You're a bright woman and have done some reading, didn't you encounter slavery in Shakespeare and your mythology?"

"Well, yes, but that doesn't justify it."

"I'm not trying to justify it. You've got to remember that there have been slaves from the beginning of history and probably always will be. Anyway, we're getting into politics and I promised your father that's something I wouldn't discuss."

"Okay," said Peggy, noticing a strained pitch in Garrett's voice. "I didn't mean to do that. I was just curious about your life. It seems so different from what I remember as a young girl in Indiana before we moved here."

"Why did your family come to Crossrock?" quizzed Garrett. "Why come to a sinful slave state when you were in a state with abolitionist politics agreeable to your own beliefs?"

"Father thought there was a good business opportunity here since it was a big, new state. He figured the politics of slavery would be resolved by men acting rationally.

In 1861 he learned it was an irrational world."

"So did most other people."

A man and wife entered the store for some groceries, interrupting the conversation. Garrett was glad, too. He had never seen Peggy this inquisitive. Maybe her proclaimed wish that he stay had opened her mind to her ignorance about this man who had walked into her life eight weeks ago.

When the couple left, Peggy turned to Garrett, wanting to resume the conversation. She was, however, uncertain whether or not Garrett wanted to talk any more. She knew she had touched a sensitive nerve when she made her comment about slavery. It was not intended, but she had heard her father's opinions on the iniquities of slavery too often to avoid responding instinctively as she did. Despite her uneasiness about further conversation, Peggy did want to pry a little more since she might not have another opportunity without her father's presence. When her father was feeling better and back at work, he would have put a stop to her questions.

"Could I ask you another question?" Peggy smiled.

"Boy, you really are as curious as a cat today. What's brought all this on?"

"Oh, I don't know. Maybe I'm just tired of reading my books and want a little conversation."

"I sure don't know what to make of it because it was several weeks after I worked here before you would even speak to me, except when you had no other choice. Now you're wanting to talk about my past and everything that has happened to me since I was born. Well, what do you want to know this time?"

"How'd you injure your arm?" she asked boldly.

"You're only the second person to ask me that since I left home. Did you know that?"

"I'm sorry if . . ."

"Most people think they know and don't even bother to ask," said Garrett, not waiting for Peggy's apology. "And most people probably do know because there are a lot of lame men walking around now, as a result of the war. If you ask one, then you know how all of them were injured."

"But yours?"

"I was riding away from a Union supply train after a raid when I got shot in the left shoulder. I knew I had been hit, but the sensations were so odd that I didn't think it was serious. As it turned out, it was one of those freak wounds that often occur when thousands of men are getting shot.

"Another three inches lower and the bullet would most certainly have struck my heart, killing me. Another three inches higher and it would have passed clean over my shoulder. As it was, it was a clean wound, except that it damaged the nerves to my arm. I couldn't move it from the moment I was shot to now and never will again.

"Lots of men came out of the war with only stumps for arms. I got out with an arm more useless than a stump. At the time, I thought it was the worst tragedy of my life. Then I got home to a family that no longer existed and the injury seemed almost meaningless."

"I guess I've always gotten my idea of war from my books. In the literature the warriors either die gloriously or return to their loved ones whole."

"Your books," said Garrett, "don't even come close to telling you about the mutilated survivors because that doesn't make a good story. Books don't tell you the truth about war because it is not pretty. The agony, the waste, the cowardice and most of all the death. Many on both sides came away much more disfigured than me and went through greater agony to get that way, but at least we survived. Thousands weren't

165

that lucky."

"Are you sorry you fought; I mean was it worth it?"

"I fought for what I believed. At the time it seemed important and maybe it would still seem important had I not lost my family. You see, the things I was fighting for, I lost anyway. So, no, it wasn't worth it, but I would probably do it again because you don't know until the end whether it will be worth it or not. Was it worth losing Tom?"

"Maybe it was worth it to his country, but it wasn't worth it for his family. It changed our existence, too drastically, too suddenly."

"It was a sad time, the war was, and I guess it scarred most people that it touched. That was a reason I wanted to get away from it, move west where there are fewer reminders of what happened."

"This is depressing. Let's talk about something else. I've got one more question to ask you. Do you mind?"

"Well, nothing has stopped you yet. Why couldn't you talk about the weather for a while?"

"No, this is nowhere like what we've been talking about or what I've asked you before," she defended herself. "Do you like parties?"

"What brought on that question? It's been a while since I have been to a party," answered Garrett. "We didn't have many in the cavalry, but the ones I remember before the war were tolerably pleasurable. Why?"

"My birthday is a week from today and I just thought it might be fun to have a little celebration. It would be small — Father, me, Billy and you, if you'll come. Will you?"

"As I recall, I don't have any other engagements that night," said Garrett. "I guess I can make it, if I'm invited. I'm sure Murphy will be tickled to see me there. Have you asked him about this?"

"No, but it is my birthday and I can ask who I please. I want you to be there, that's all."

"Okay, I accept your invitation. You just tell me the time and I'll make it on the dot without borrowing your father's watch again."

"Look, you've redeemed yourself by getting his watch back. You won't hear anything from me about that."

"I'll be there then and we'll have a grand time. Say, how old will you be?"

"Nineteen," she said.

"Goodness," Garrett answered with a twinkle in his steel-gray eyes. "You're almost an old maid."

Peggy just turned up her nose and began

straightening up a cluttered counter. Garrett, too, had work to do and he went in the back room to bring the ledgers up to date. Both stayed busy until Peggy decided it was time to leave and check on her father.

Garrett was pleased at her invitation and decided he would give her something special for a birthday gift. But what that would be, Garrett did not know. Were she not the storekeeper's daughter, there would have been plenty of things to buy for her in the store. But Peggy was familiar with the combs and the brushes, the ribbons and the aprons, and the brooches and the lace. No other place within thirty miles had a selection as good as the Dobbs General Store, Garrett thought. Even if it were otherwise, he would not have the time to go looking for a special gift. There were so many things he would liked to have given her, but they could not be found shy of New Orleans or St. Louis. Surely, Garrett thought, he could come up with something that she would enjoy. When customers or chores did not command his attention, he puzzled over what to give her.

After a day's worry, Garrett still had no ideas he was pleased with. Nothing seemed appropriate for Peggy Dobbs. When she and her father were in the store in the days preceding her birthday, Garrett seemed pre-occupied, almost oblivious to the presence of the others. Finally, he settled on the pretty tortoise shell hairbrush that was the envy of many women who did their wishing in the store. He was not totally satisfied with his choice, but he decided he could give her something else, if anything special ever came to mind.

Three nights before her birthday, Garrett was trying to go to sleep in the back room of the store, his thoughts still on the gift for Peggy. He would have been satisfied to get her another book, were that possible. But even if it were, she probably already had a copy. Deciding to get up and look on the bookshelf across the room, Garrett lit a lamp. As he looked over the books which covered the four shelves of the bookcase, he realized that several of Shakespeare's plays were there. Then it struck him. Why not write down a few passages of Shakespeare that she might enjoy? That would appeal to Peggy; he knew it would. His mind made up, Garrett wracked his brain trying to remember some of the passages he had enjoyed while at the academy or some he had used in corresponding with his wife. It was a long process that kept Garrett up later than he thought it would. He spent much of the time trying to locate the passages in the plays or in finding new ones. He had found three when he realized how late it was. Returning to bed after blowing out the lamp, Garrett was pleased with his decision. He felt confident that Peggy would enjoy the gift. The next night after work, Garrett took some paper at the back desk where he did the ledger work and with pen in hand began to transcribe the quotations. In a fine, steady hand, he worked for an hour on a product of penmanship that would have made his academy master proud.

On death, an occurrence that had recently shaped both of their lives, he took some lines from *Hamlet:*

Thou know'st tis common; all that lives must die, Passing through nature to eternity.

On beauty, Garrett took two lines from *Henry VIII:*

The fairest hand I ever touch'd! Till now I never knew thee.

Finally, on love, Garrett copied down a single line from *The Twelfth Night:*

170

Love sought is good, but given unsought is better.

Pleased with the result, Garrett allowed the ink to dry and then folded the paper and placed it in an envelope. He wrote Peggy's name on the front. Now he was satisfied, and after hiding the envelope in the desk, he blew out the lamp and retired.

The day of Peggy's birthday brought a ferociously cold norther that made even a brief walk outside intolerably long. For a day which held so much promise, Garrett was disappointed in the weather. He had wanted one of those pleasant winter days he had come to enjoy so much during his stay in Crossrock. But it was not to be for the wind whipped through the street, scattering dust in the air and rattling the store, as if nature was against all obstacles built by man. Garrett shivered as he awoke and stepped out from the covers that morning. He went outside to fetch enough wood to bring the dying fire in the stove back to life. As he warmed himself in front of the rejuvenated fire, he looked across the street at the darkened boarding house. Several of the wooden slats that had been nailed across the doors and windows of the building had come loose during the night and were blowing with the breeze, making a hammering noise that sounded more like the building was being constructed rather than gradually being blown apart by nature. As Garrett stood watching the building across the street, he was surprised to see Dobbs and Peggy coming toward the store. Peggy was wearing a heavy coat, but Dobbs's coat was a lighter one and quite worn. Surely Dobbs had a better coat than that, Garrett thought to himself.

"I wasn't sure I would see either of you on a day like this," said Garrett as they hurried in the door. "I believe this is the coldest morning since I've been here."

"Cold it is," said Dobbs. "There's no doubt about that. The wind makes it just miserable to be out, but I haven't worked that much over the last few weeks and thought I had better come in for a change. Peg, she has to get a few things before she goes back home and gets ready for our little party."

"How does it feel to be an old lady now?" Garrett teased Peggy.

"I ought not to do this after that insult," said Peggy, as she grabbed his right hand to button the cuff on his sleeve, "but if I don't, it'll probably never get done. Where did you learn your manners, anyway? You could refrain from your insults."

"It's hard not to be insulting when it's this cold."

"Well, you'd better try, or I just might take back my invitation for you tonight."

"Yes, ma'am," said Garrett with a sweeping bow. "It is nice weather we're having, isn't it?"

"Oh," cried Peggy in frustration, "quit being so silly. Goodness, I want to get what I came after and get out of here. I've got a thousand things to do for tonight and staying here discussing things with you is not accomplishing much."

Gathering up her needs, Peggy departed the store, leaving the two men behind.

"She's really excited today," said Dobbs. "It's been a long time since I have seen her this way. I'm glad to see it in her."

"She was a bit feisty, wasn't she?" said Garrett. "Yes, she's some girl, or I guess I should say woman. Oh, I forgot to ask what time she wanted me to get there."

"I believe about seven o'clock," said her father. "You need to borrow my watch again?"

Garrett laughed, "No, sir, not after what it caused last time. I would hate to spoil her birthday party."

"Go ahead, if you want to borrow it."

"Nope," said Garrett. "Without it, I'll have a good excuse if I am late. And, if I decide to get there early to fluster her, she can't say I did it intentionally."

"Say, you're in sort of a feisty mood yourself, today," Dobbs said to Garrett. "I just hope Bill isn't or I am going to have my hands full tonight."

"Don't worry about me. Say, why don't you go on home. It's not going to be busy today with weather like this and I can take care of it. Peggy will probably need your help more than me."

"I may just do that," said Dobbs. "You know, though, I came here for something and right now it has just completely slipped my mind. I guess I will go on home and maybe I can think of it there."

"Well, if I can help, let me know."

Dobbs put on his ragged coat and left the store, pausing out in the street opposite the abandoned boarding house to wrap his coat tighter around himself. Then he hurried home.

Not a single other person came in the store that day, and time seemed to drag by. Garrett was fidgety again, another case of his war nerves. He was nervous, too, about the gifts he would give Peggy. He was both proud and ashamed to be giving her the hairbrush. She deserved something better, but that was about the best available. Garrett was actually scared about the envelope he had for her. Perhaps she would take it the wrong way; he knew Murphy sure would, but then maybe Murphy was right. Although Murphy had shaken hands with him and agreed to be friends, that was before Peggy had shown interest in Garrett. Now, Murphy's failure ever to come by the store when Garrett was around seemed ominous. Perhaps he was wrong, but Garrett still did not trust Murphy, particularly if the former Union soldier realized that Garrett was growing attached to Peggy.

At closing time, Garrett was relieved to lock up the door and ready himself to attend the party. He wore the workclothes that Dobbs had given him, instead of the outfit that had once been his uniform. It would be more polite, he thought, not to antagonize anyone tonight and risk spoiling Peggy's birthday celebration.

Finally, Garrett could wait no longer. He knew it was early; but he decided he was ready to go. First, he put the envelope with Peggy's name on it in his shirt pocket. The hairbrush wrapped in foil he put in his pants pocket. With the winds still howling and the sun now down, taking what little warmth it had provided during the day, Garrett decided he was not going to leave his gray greatcoat behind just to avoid exacerbating Murphy's Union distemper. Putting it on and buttoning it up, Garrett grabbed his gray hat and pulled it down over his head. Opening the door and then locking it behind him, he stepped out into the darkness of the night. He took a final glance at the store and through the window he could see the glow of the well-fed stove, which seemed to light up the inside of the building. It was comforting to know that when he returned for bed, it would be warm inside. But that satisfaction did not shield him from the bitterly cold wind that seemed to cut into his face. He walked hastily from the store toward the Dobbs house where lighted windows acted as beacons, giving him the right course.

Quickly he walked to the distant house where he pounded on the door. Dobbs opened up, allowing Garrett and some of the cold wind to slip in behind him.

"That's bad weather out there."

"Come in this warm house, Morgan," said Dobbs. "You're early."

"I got tired of waiting and figured it would only get colder the longer I stayed."

"Well, good for you, it was getting a little

boring around here with Peggy so busy. I'm glad to see you came early."

"Murphy here yet?"

"No, he had some work to do out at his place, or so he said yesterday. With the weather like this, I thought he might have just come on in to town, but as stubborn as he is he probably went ahead with his chores. Anyway, he's supposed to be here by seven. In this weather, though, it wouldn't surprise me if he were a bit late."

"Where's Peggy? I don't hear her stirring in the kitchen."

"She's been so excited all day that I don't think anything can slow her down until this is over. She's in her room getting dressed and that's as still as she has been all day."

Then the ever-frowning Dobbs grabbed Garrett by the arm and pulled him over in the corner and whispered, "You know I forgot something when I came to the store today?"

"You've remembered?"

"Yes, sir, Morgan, I feel like an old fool, but I've remembered. It was her birthday gift. How I forgot I don't know, but it sure did slip my mind until this afternoon. Whenever Peggy gets dressed, I'm going to go back and get it."

"How about if I go get it for you?"

"No, that would never do. Peggy has been so excited all day and anxious for company that she'd be disappointed to find I was still here while you went to do my errand."

"It wouldn't take but a minute, if I left right now."

"No, it's settled. I'll go get it and you just stay and visit with Peg. Anyway, I might wait there a couple minutes and come back with Bill when I see him pass. That way, if he's late, she can't be mad at him since he had to wait on me."

"Whatever you think is best."

"Okay then."

The men turned as they heard the opening of a door from Dobbs's bedroom. It was Peggy. She was wearing a longsleeve white blouse with a high-top collar and lace down the front. She wore a long, black skirt which almost touched the floor. It was simple attire, but that made it all the more striking on Peggy. She entered the room and waited a moment for Garrett to speak.

"You look very nice tonight," he said.

"Thank you. Do I still look like an old woman?"

"Not at all. You look very pretty and not a day over nineteen tonight. I take back my earlier comment."

"Well, are you going to take off your coat

and stay or are you leaving?" she asked.

"I'm staying," said Garrett, as he took off his hat and coat.

"But I'm going," said her father, "I forgot something at the store and I need to go get it."

"Wouldn't you know this would happen on my birthday?"

"Look, I'll get my coat and I won't be long."

"Here," said Garrett, "use mine. It ought to keep you warmer than that one of yours. On a night like this you're going to need all the warmth you can get."

Dobbs stood there sheepishly looking at that gray coat.

"Maybe you're right," he said softly, "though I never thought I'd wear Confederate gray."

"You're about my height so it ought to fit," said Garrett, as he tossed the greatcoat to Dobbs.

Putting it on, Dobbs turned to Peggy. "What do you think?"

"I believe I like you in blue better," she said.

"Well, I guess I do too, but this is a warm coat."

"Take my hat, too," said Garrett, "and it'll keep that head warm. It won't hurt you."

Once again Dobbs followed the instructions and when he placed it on his head, Garrett felt he almost saw a sheepish grin on Dobbs's usually frowning face. They laughed and then out into the cold Dobbs went on his errand, leaving Peggy and Garrett alone.

After he had left, Dobbs pulled the envelope with Peggy's name on it from out of his shirt and the wrapped brush from his pants pocket.

"Here, these are for you."

"Thank you," she said, "that's very thoughtful. Let me put these on the bookshelf and I'll open them later."

"I've looked forward to this ever since you asked me to come," said Garrett.

"And, I've looked forward to having you, too. I just wish Billy would get here and Father had remembered to take care of his business earlier so he could've stayed here. That makes me angry, his forgetfulness."

"In defense of your father, it could be that your birthday is the cause of his extra trip."

"Oh," said Peggy with an embarrassed gulp, "but what about Billy? He could've made an effort to get here earlier. He makes me so mad sometimes."

"Well, I can't tell you about Murphy. I'm just trying to look out for myself."

"And Father, you do look out after him don't you?"

"In a way."

"Well, I've noticed that and it doesn't go unappreciated. Say, come in the kitchen and I'll show you what I've done."

Taking Garrett by the arm and then buttoning his cuff, Peggy led him into the adjacent room. The aroma of food was most tantalizing. Garrett could hardly wait to sit down and enjoy the meal. One thing he had learned from all the food that Peggy had brought him was that she was a good cook. He relished the idea of eating another meal of hers straight off the stove.

"I've worked all day for this and I hope it's good," she said.

"It certainly smells good to me."

Just as she was about to uncover one of the black pots on the stove, Peggy let out a shrill yell.

"There in the corner," she said, "is that darn mouse I've been trying to kill. Help me get him."

Grabbing a broom, Peggy rushed the corner and let loose a terrific swat which missed the mouse. Garrett picked up a poker from the stove woodbox and offered reinforcements. The mouse made a feint to the right and then ran left past Garrett and out of the kitchen into the sitting room.

"Hurry," said Peggy, "I don't want him to get away this time."

Leading the way, Peggy charged after the rodent with Garrett right behind her. After chasing it from under a chair, the two once again trapped the mouse in an empty corner of the house.

Garrett raised his poker for a swing, but was reluctant to strike too hard with the heavy poker. Nonetheless, he let go with a cautious swing which missed the mark and sent the mouse scurrying, neither left nor right this time, but straight at Peggy's skirt.

"Aaaah," screamed Peggy, dropping the broom and hoisting her skirt halfway up her calves.

While the mouse made its final escape, Garrett doubled over laughing. It was not a gentle laughter, but an uproarious commotion that at first angered Peggy. When Garrett sat down still chuckling heartily, Peggy began to grin, then to break out in laughter herself. Finally, she plopped down on the couch beside him.

They looked at each other with tears of laughter almost running down their faces. And then, as if they had planned it, both suddenly stopped laughing. Still gazing in each other's eyes, they seemed at peace.

Then Garrett reached over and kissed her on the lips. Peggy did not flinch, but instead wrapped her arms around him and returned his passionate kisses. For a moment, they broke their silent kiss and looked in each other's eyes once again, as if to say it was okay. Garrett was shocked at what he had done, but he knew from the look in Peggy's eyes that she would not spurn his advances.

He sat there enjoying the fragrance of her hair and the warmth of her breath and the softness of her lips. It was a moment of tenderness that Garrett treasured. He pulled her body closer to his, enjoying the touch of her breasts against his chest, and kissed her even harder.

Suddenly, there was a flurry of noise outside, a yell for Peggy and the hasty opening of the front door. It was Murphy. And for a moment, the massive man just stood there, silently glaring at the two who had had little time to do more than break their embrace, much less hide their intentions. Garrett could see the hate welling in the other man's eyes. Murphy now knew how Garrett felt that night he had seen Peggy kissing him in the kitchen window.

"Peggy, come quick," Murphy said after his stunned pause. "Your father's been shot."

"No!" Peggy jumped up from the couch and raced past Murphy in the door. Murphy stood for a moment just glaring at Garrett and then turned to follow the girl. His long strides brought him beside the terrified woman as she raced to the store. Garrett, stunned for a moment by the untimely interruption and the horrible news, bounded up from the couch and ran after them.

The wind was howling and the cold cut right through their clothes, but the coatless Peggy and Garrett were oblivious to the discomfort. They were warmed by the anger generated by the shooting of Dobbs. Decker and his boys would pay for this, thought Garrett, who knew no one else would have done such a cowardly thing.

Up ahead at the store, Garrett could see a circle of about a dozen men around a prone figure. It was Dobbs, silent and still. Murphy had caught Peggy and ran with her to the store front. Clearing a patch among those that had gathered around the body on the plank sidewalk, Murphy held Peggy's hand as she silently approached the body. When she saw that it was indeed her father, she bent down.

"Father, oh Father, can't you talk to me?" she sobbed, as she lifted his head and cradled it against her breast. "Don't leave me now like Mother and Tom did. Please . . ."

She trailed off into tears and could say nothing more. Murphy removed her dead father from her arms and reverently picked him up. Then, opening the door with Dobbs's key still in the lock, Murphy carried the old man through the store and into the back room where he laid the body on Garrett's cot. Garrett had followed Murphy in, lighting a lamp once inside. Taking the light into the backroom, Garrett saw the strange pallor of death on the storekeeper's face. Oddly, though, there was also a gentle smile across Dobbs's face. It was the only time Garrett had ever seen such a smile. Perhaps it was in anticipation of Peggy's birthday party.

"Get Peggy out of here," Murphy told Garrett, who immediately obliged.

Out in the store, Garrett found about a dozen whispering people, including many of the men who frequented the Dobbs store for the old man's warm stove and his political discussions. There, too, was the saloonkeeper Benton and his wife.

"Come here, dear," said Maude Benton to Peggy. "Stand by the stove and warm up. You must be freezing."

Maude Benton took Peggy from Garrett's grasp and backed her toward the stove. Peggy had regained her composure. Now she stood with a blank, frightened look on her face, as if she realized something terrible had happened but could not fully comprehend what.

Garrett turned and went to the back room again. There he found Murphy taking the gray coat off the body.

"Damn you," said Murphy when Garrett reappeared. "What was he doing in your coat?"

"I loaned it to him to come back here for something he left behind."

"You sent him to his death is what you did," Murphy charged. "Nobody here would want to kill him, not even Decker's boys. It was you they wanted, dammit."

When Murphy finally got the coat off, he held it up. There in the back, just to the left side of center below the shoulder blade, was a bullet hole with a crimson border.

Garrett's hat was missing. In all likelihood, it had been knocked off Dobbs's head when he was shot and carried away by the wind.

"You've brought nothing but trouble since you arrived here," said Murphy. "Now you've sent an old man to his grave, a man

186

that never harmed anybody."

Garrett said nothing, for what could he say? He just stood there waiting for Murphy to challenge him over his brief embrace with Peggy, but the big man said nothing about it.

"Tell me," said Garrett, "did you see anything when you rode into town?"

"Sure, I did," Murphy huffed. "I saw his body lying there with a couple people around him."

"No, did you see who fired the shot or where it came from?"

"I saw and heard nothing except the wind until I got near the store. Some of the men there said they heard a shot and went out to check. They found his body."

"He must of been shot by a sniper somewhere in the boarding house," said Garrett as he looked out the door of the back room through the front window at the vacant building across the street. "That had to be it."

"Well, why don't you go over and see. Maybe they'll get who they were aiming for this time. If you don't come back, it would suit me fine."

Garrett turned and walked out of the back room into the front of the store. There he saw Maude Benton and others comforting

Peggy. Feeling helpless and unwanted, he opened the door and walked out into the street to be enveloped by the cold, gusting winds. Without his coat now, Garrett shivered with every blast of air. He had to find shelter, but he was unsure where. He might have stayed at the store, but that would only have antagonized Murphy further. There was no way he could go to the Dobbs house after what had happened. If the Bentons put Peggy up for the night, as he had heard them suggest, it would not be appropriate for him to stay there. He lost track of where he was going as he worried over where to stay the night. When he finally did look up, he was outside the livery stable. He would stay there.

Going inside, Garrett was accosted by a voice.

"Who is it and state your business, unless you want a load of buckshot for your efforts?"

"It's Morgan Garrett. Is that you Holcomb?"

"Yeah," said Holcomb, who lit a lamp when he recognized Garrett's voice. "Sorry, about challenging you, but I wanted to be certain who it was after the killing."

"I understand. Say, you once told me I could stay the night in your stable. That offer still stand?"

"Sure it does, although you sure picked a cold night to take me up on it."

"Don't figure I'm much wanted by Peggy Dobbs and particularly by Murphy after the old man's death."

"You didn't shoot him, though."

"No, but Dobbs was wearing my coat and hat when he was shot. I'm to blame because that bullet was meant for me."

"The shot came from the boarding house."

"That's what I think."

"That's what I know," said Holcomb. "I saw the flash from the shot. Somebody was up in a second-floor window. Thought I saw someone ride away when the commotion started."

"Could you tell who it was?"

"Not for sure. Of course, if they was after you, it was probably Decker or Skinner."

"That's what I think, but I'd like to know which one. If I ever find out, I'll kill him."

Chapter 8

A small group stood silently at the brown, barren cemetery as the wooden coffin was lowered into the cold earth. Garrett, the only coatless mourner, stood behind the small funeral gathering on that cold, still morning two sunrises after Dobbs's death. Although Garrett had seen a lot of death, too much death, in the months that led him to Crossrock, this was the first funeral ceremony he remembered attending since before the war. He had been absent from even the simple ceremony that put his wife and sons to rest.

Now, in this ugly spot in Texas, Garrett felt he was burying another part of himself. He owed Dobbs more than he could ever have repaid even if the old man had lived. With his death though, Garrett could only think of one thing that would settle his debt to Dobbs — to find and kill his murderer. After that, Garrett suspected he would carry out his earlier plans, plans temporarily shelved by Peggy, to move on west with the spring. Garrett didn't think it would take him the seven weeks before spring was due to identify the killer. After that score was settled, Garrett would move on. Although he hadn't talked to Peggy since her father's death, he doubted she would want him to operate the store for her now. Sure, there was the need, greater than ever, but Garrett's unintentional hand in her father's death had probably soured their tenuous relationship.

Garrett watched Peggy, who had Murphy at her side, for he had not seen her since her father's death. While his glazed eyes watched the young woman, Garrett shivered visibly. He had not gone back to the store for his greatcoat, and, even if he had, he would not have worn it with Dobbs's blood on it to the old man's funeral. Thus, the bitter chill was painful to the Alabaman. Even so, he was so immersed in his own deliberations that he failed to realize when the simple ceremony had ended. As he stood there, others turned around and walked silently past him, not so much ignoring him intentionally, but desiring to get back to their warm homes. Peggy, who was given condolences by everyone, leaned over the open grave for a final look at the stark pine coffin. That done, she turned around, Murphy still at her side.

"Morgan," she said, but before she could finish, Garrett interrupted.

"I'm sorry, Peggy, I really am. I asked your father to let me run back to the store for him, but he insisted he wanted to do it. If only I hadn't given him the coat."

"Where is your coat? You really shouldn't be out in this weather without it."

"I never got it back from the store and I couldn't wear it to your father's funeral even if I did."

"But haven't you been back to the store since Father was shot?"

"No, I haven't. I thought it best I stay away."

"Then where have you been staying in this horrible, cold weather?"

"Holcomb has been letting me sleep at the stable. I just didn't think I'd really be wanted at the store."

"Whoever gave you that idea?" Peggy inquired, then answered herself as she looked at the stony Murphy. "You're not to blame for Father's death, no matter what anyone says. Now I'm going to need you more than ever."

"No, you're not," said Murphy, who had

maintained a raging silence until then. "I'll be able to help you out at the store. You won't have to pay me anything either."

"Sure, Billy, you'll be a big help. You don't know anything about working at the store. You've told me before that you couldn't stand to be cooped up inside like a chicken for the entire day. Anyway, how will you get your place in shape and that house built you're always telling me about, if you spend all your time at the store?"

"I won't spend all my time there. I can work half a day at the place and half here."

"That's smart because then it will take you twice as long to get anything done at the place and probably make it twice as difficult for me to get any work done at the store. No, it's not going to be that way because Morgan can help out. He knows what he's doing and he's a good hand."

Garrett said nothing as Peggy argued with Murphy. Unlike the first time he had seen Peggy, she was now defending the need for keeping him at the store.

"I still don't like it and I don't care for him. He knows that. Don't you Garrett?"

"You've made yourself plain on that point, Murphy."

"Enough, you two. I've got no choice and neither do you. You're all the family I've got

193

left. I can't handle all this myself, at least for now. I suspect we are in for some more trouble with the Decker boys and I don't want us fighting among ourselves. Now come on, let's go back home before Morgan freezes to death."

Silently, the trio marched back the two hundred yards to Crossrock and the store. Only the sounds of each breath broke the stillness that had settled over the land. Peggy walked between the two men, holding a hand of each. Despite Peggy's plea, Garrett still felt uncomfortable because of Murphy. There was no way he could stay around that huge, stubborn man very much longer. Garrett's resolve grew even firmer. Once Dobbs's murderer was dead, he would leave Crossrock forever, even if spring had not arrived. He just couldn't accept the possibility that Peggy was going to marry Murphy. He was too oafish for her refined tastes, Garrett thought. But then again, maybe Texas was no place for Peggy Dobbs. The land was too primitive, too dry, too rugged for a young woman like her.

Maybe she could grow to love the land, but Garrett could not understand her affection for Murphy. The massive man with roughhewn edges was not handsome, although he was not ugly, either. Perhaps plain was the best description of his looks, dominated by his red hair and ruddy complexion. It certainly was not Murphy's education, for while he could read and write, he was nowhere near as skillful as Peggy. Murphy was a solid worker, Garrett admitted, but that was all the Alabaman would give him credit for.

Both men were galled, having to share Peggy's attention as they walked back to town. For each of the jealous men, the other's presence meant that no conversation would be attempted, no glances exchanged. Each resented the other's imposition. By contrast, Peggy seemed contented and safe as she walked between the two men. When they reached the Dobbs store, which had been closed since the death of its owner, Garrett let go of Peggy's hand and retrieved his key from his pocket. It was almost as cold inside as out because the stove fire, the fire which Garrett had built before Dobbs's fateful return, had long since died. Once inside, Peggy turned to her companions and began to give orders.

"Billy, go out back and get some firewood. Bring enough in to last through tomorrow. Morgan, you find your coat or wrap yourself up in one of those quilts in the back until we can get the fire going."

It was a decisiveness which Garrett had not seen in Peggy before. Unlike the past, she seemed to be in command of the situation, unafraid to make a decision and to demand its execution. Frankly, Garrett was surprised. He had expected her girlish dependence to be heightened by the loss of her father. Instead, Peggy appeared steady and controlled. This unexpected change in Peggy pleased Garrett, who went to the back room for cover as ordered, because it meant she could handle his leaving when that time came. Garrett found his coat on the floor where Murphy had tossed it after removing it from Dobbs. He picked it up, but did not want Peggy to see him in it so he laid it on the bed and smoothed out the wrinkles as best he could. As he did, he could hear Murphy mumbling at the wood pile out the back door. Garrett grabbed a quilt and stuck one corner in his mouth and reached around his back with his good right hand to pull the blanket over his shoulders. That done, he grabbed the two corners of the quilt at his chest and walked out front.

"Come here," said Peggy when he reappeared. "Let me button that right sleeve for you. You've probably gone around the last two days with it unbuttoned."

As she buttoned it, Garrett heard Murphy

struggling to open the back door with his armload of firewood. Finally, the door came open, just as Peggy was pulling the blanket around Garrett for more warmth.

Seeing the two so close to each other, Murphy could retain his rage no more. Dropping the firewood with a startling crash, Murphy rushed up front from the back room.

Just as Garrett turned to see what had happened, Murphy shoved him with a force that sent him sprawling across the floor.

"Stop, Billy, stop," yelled Peggy.

But Murphy was deaf to those plaintive cries. All he could see in his mind was Garrett holding Peggy and kissing her two nights ago. As Garrett stood up to defend himself, Murphy let loose with a fearsome punch that seemed to explode when it hit Garrett. Surprisingly, though, Garrett remained on his feet long enough for Murphy to get in one more blow, this one a smashing punch to the nose. Bloodied, Garrett fell to the floor, sprawled out in a murky daze with a puffy eye and a mouth and nose that oozed blood.

Peggy continued yelling, but to no avail. After the second punch, she jumped on Billy's back and grabbed him around the neck, trying to keep him off his downed

197

rival. The strong Murphy seemed almost oblivious to her presence as he stood glaring over Garrett.

"If you ever touch her again, I'll kill you," he shouted, then repeated the threat to make sure the semiconscious Garrett understood him.

"Please stop, Billy," Peggy cried. "He's done nothing that I didn't let him do. Don't say you're going to kill him. Just stop, leave and I will see you at the house later."

As Murphy backed away, Peggy let go and slipped off his back to the floor.

"You just remember what I told you, Garrett. You may work here, but I'm not going to like it and I'd better not ever catch you holding her again."

With that said, Murphy strode out the front door, slamming it behind him with the strength he would have preferred to use on Garrett.

"Morgan, Morgan," Peggy pleaded, "are you okay? I'm sorry, I didn't know he was so angry. I tried to stop him, but he's so big. Tell me you are okay."

Garrett could only nod. His thoughts were still jumbled by the jarring blows to his head. His vision was blurry and his face was bloody. Peggy tried to clean him up as best she could and then she helped him to his cot in the backroom.

"You just lay here and I'll bring in some more firewood and build you a fire."

Garrett was too weak to object and he did as he was told. After several trips by Peggy from the back door, past his bed to the stove and back, Garrett could smell the aroma of burning wood and feel the sharpness in the air gradually being dulled by the warmth from the stove.

As the building heated up, Garrett slipped off into a deep sleep. It was the first good sleep he had had since Dobbs was shot, although it was not without its pain because of the beating from Murphy. At times, Garrett thought he felt the warm hands of Peggy brushing his face, but he was not sure whether he was just dreaming or not. When he did begin to stir, his thoughts were clearer, although he had a terrible headache. As he opened his eyes and they began to focus, he saw Peggy seated on a stool beside his cot.

"Are you better?"

"Little bit. How long did I sleep?"

"About an hour or so, I guess. I really lost track of time because I was worried for you. I'll apologize for Billy because I'm sure he's sorry for this."

"He won't be sorry. He's held a grudge

199

against me from the day I saw him and it won't matter what you tell him."

"He just seems to get more stubborn every day. He never used to be like this."

"Maybe he never saw anyone else kiss you before."

"I guess not, but he doesn't tell me who I can kiss."

With that, she leaned over and planted a gentle kiss on Garrett's lips.

"See what I mean?"

"I just hope your friend Murphy isn't looking in the window because he seems to take those kisses out on me."

"Maybe so, but it won't happen again," she said with fire rising in her voice. "If he ever does strike you again, I'll tell him to stay away from me. Look, you two can't be fighting all the time because I need you, both of you."

Garrett did not respond. He told himself it was his headache, but really he knew that he did not want to tell Peggy he still planned to leave in the spring. There was no way he could stand to be around Murphy much longer than the cold weather would force him to.

"I know you must be tired and need a good night's sleep," said Peggy, breaking the uncomfortable silence, so I'm going on home. I plan to open the store up tomorrow just as Father always did. Will you be able by then?"

"Probably, if your boyfriend doesn't decide he wants to hit me again."

"You just worry about feeling better and I'll worry about keeping him off you. Understand?"

"Whatever you say, Miss Dobbs, because you're the boss," said Garrett with a grin that told Peggy he would be better by morning.

"And don't call me Miss Dobbs again or you may be looking for a new job!"

"Yes, ma'am, Miss Dobbs," Garrett laughed feebly.

"Goodbye, Mr. Garrett," Peggy retorted as she strode out of the backroom and the building.

In his solitude, Garrett sought sleep for his aching head, but his thoughts were still on Peggy and his confused emotions about her and Crossrock. Although it was better than two hours before Garrett finally managed to go off to sleep, it was not quite dark when he did. He slept soundly until some internal time clock aroused him for a day's work.

The first day back at work was uneventful, although it seemed so strange not to

201

have Dobbs around. Garrett felt as if Dobbs would walk in the front door any minute and take up his accustomed routine. Undoubtedly, that would never happen, but Garrett could not shake that feeling for some reason. Neither did it help on another day when Garrett was moving some goods around in the back room when he spotted a dress box with some ribbon around it. On top of the rectangular dress box was scrawled "Happy Birthday, Peg." This was what Dobbs had returned for the night of his death. At first, Garrett was tempted to open the box and see what the old man had given his daughter for a gift. But Garrett stopped himself from lifting the lid. It was as if it would be disrespectful to the dead man. For an instant Garrett thought of taking the box out front to Peggy, but something held him back. The timing just didn't seem right. It was still too close to her father's death. Ever since her breakdown, Peggy had maintained her composure with a strength that had amazed Garrett. Now the Alabaman was hesitant to present her the gift for fear it would upset that steady composure. Instead of taking it to her, Garrett placed the box back where he had found it and returned to his work with his secret intact.

Like her father before her, Peggy arrived at work each morning precisely at seven o'clock. The store was opened an hour later and Peggy was generally there most of the day, except for the thirty minutes she would take for lunch and the occasional errands, both business and personal, which she ran. Since she no longer had her father to feed, Peggy did not cook a lunch, as she was a light eater, evident by her slender figure. Garrett really missed the lunches she once brought.

Rather than do without his noon meal, as he had often done when he first arrived in Crossrock, Garrett took to eating each day at Benton's saloon. The fare had improved some since that first meal Garrett had eaten there. The one thing that had not changed, though, was the amusing bickering between the saloonkeeper and his wife, Maude. So each day with his lunch, Garrett witnessed the ongoing drama of the domestic life of Benton and his wife. Garrett was fond of the couple, particularly Maude Benton. She talked too much, a trait that Garrett would have despised in others, but coming from her it was almost natural and unoffensive. Garrett never minded her ramblings.

Two weeks after the store reopened for business, the normal ramblings of Maude

Benton came to an instant halt when Garrett walked in the door of the saloon for lunch. Immediately, Garrett saw the reason why for there in the corner alone at a table was Ed Skinner. The eyes of the two men met with a hateful exchange.

"Barkeep," said the drunken Skinner, "bring me another whiskey and give a drink to Lefty there. I want to buy him his last drink."

Seeing the state of Skinner, Garrett was not too worried about a confrontation with guns or fists. Still Garrett was glad he had worn his holster and his .44 revolver. Although he did not expect to use the weapon, it was a good feeling, nonetheless, having it handy. Ignoring Skinner, Garrett took a plate from the counter and helped himself to the food lined up on platters beside the stack of plates.

Skinner, though, continued to throw insults at Garrett, who chose to ignore them because he needed to eat his meal and get back to the store so Peggy could take her lunch break. Further, too many times in the past he had had a confrontation with Decker or some of his boys in the Benton Saloon and he did not want another brawl there.

"Barkeep," shouted Skinner, "I've finished my drink and need another. Bring me one.

Say, you haven't taken Lefty his whiskey yet. Now just why not?"

Benton stammered out an incomprehensible answer, but Skinner was not sober enough to care.

"Well, before you bring me mine, barkeep, you take one over to Lefty. I want to see him drink his last whiskey."

Benton, with a helpless frown creasing his face, looked over at Garrett, as if asking what to do. Garrett smiled in return, silently giving Benton the okay to bring the drink over.

After Benton delivered the drink to Garrett, he took another one to Skinner. Maude Benton had remained strangely silent and was jolted by Garrett, who paused from his meal.

"Maude, could you bring me another piece of bread?" he asked.

She did as she was asked without saying a word. When she got to the table, Garrett whispered to her.

"How long's he been in here?"

"Better than an hour and drinking all the time."

"What about the others?" quizzed Garrett. "Have they been in here today?"

"No," said the woman softly, "I haven't seen any of them but him."

"Well, I don't like not knowing where the others are, but I'm not going to put up with him insulting me much longer."

"Now don't get yourself hurt, Morgan, just let it pass."

"Wish I could, but it's not the insults as much as it is Dobbs's death. I'm sure this bunch is the one responsible for it."

"Drink up, Lefty," shouted Skinner. "You ain't got many more days to live."

Picking up the glass of whiskey, Garrett walked over to Skinner's table.

"I've faced a lot more danger in my life than your threats," said Garrett to the drunken troublemaker. "Now you say I haven't got long to live. Do you want to settle this here and now or do you want to shut up so I can eat my meal with a little peace and quiet."

"You don't scare me, Lefty," Skinner said, rising unsteadily from his chair. "You may have one arm, but I got two good ones here."

With that Skinner raised his fists, as if he were a prize-fighter. His weaving stance, however, was one of unsteadiness, not fighting prowess, and made him an easy mark for Garrett, who for the first time since he arrived in Crossrock found himself with a decided pugilistic advantage. Ignoring an urge to floor his drunken adversary, Garrett put the whiskey glass down on Skinner's table and backed to his own.

"I don't drink with your kind," he said.

"Lefty, you're gonna regret never taking this drink because you're gonna die. Brad is gonna see to that."

"You tell your friend that I will meet him anytime in a fair fight, fists or guns. I can take him."

"You're lucky you'll get a chance to take him," said Skinner, who downed the whiskey Garrett had returned to his table and fell into his drunken muddle even further.

"What do you mean?" quizzed Garrett, whose eyes had suddenly narrowed and the gray in them glistened like sunlight off a cavalry saber.

"You're lucky to get another chance," Skinner repeated. "If you'd been wearing your coat the other night, Brad would have taken care of you."

Instantly, Garrett ran over to the drunken man and slapped Skinner as hard as he could. Recoiling from the blow, Skinner just stood there, not sure what he had said to provoke Garrett. His mind muddled from too much liquor, Skinner never realized he had fingered the murderer of Dobbs.

"You tell your friend Brad Decker that I

want to see him in town tomorrow. Tell him I plan to kill him."

Garrett then punched the drunk again.

"Do you understand my message? You tell him to come to town and to come armed because I plan to blow him off the face of the earth."

Skinner, nodding profusely, slowly backed away from the angry Garrett.

"You'd better remember to give Decker my message."

Skinner kept backing away from Garrett until he reached the door. Then he turned and ran outside.

"Morgan," said saloonkeeper Benton, "you better be careful now because Decker won't just come at you alone. He'll bring all his friends with him."

Maude Benton, though, was less cautious.

"If there's ever a man that needed killing it is that Decker," she started. "I bet he doesn't even show up in town tomorrow."

"Sure he will," retorted her husband. "You don't think he would let a one-armed man, no offense, Morgan, run him out of town. He'll be here and he'll bring his gang with him for good measure. That's why you've got to be careful. You can't beat all of them."

"Decker's the one I want," said Garrett. "As long as I can get him, the rest don't matter. His buddies won't stay around long, if he's dead."

"Maybe not, Morgan, but I would hate for you to get hurt going against those bad odds. I guess I could try to help, but I don't know if I would be of much aid to you. I'm not good with a pistol."

"I'm not asking for any help. All I want is someone to watch out for my back and yell in case they try to set me up."

"He can do that," volunteered Maude Benton, who was glowing over her husband's offer to help, but even happier over Garrett's refusal. Much as she hated Brad Decker, Maude didn't want to risk her husband in an effort to get rid of the rascal.

"Thanks," said Garrett, sitting back down to the rest of his cold meal.

Events in the saloon had helped Garrett lose track of the time. He ate his food slowly, contemplating the developments that had brought his brief stay in Crossrock to an impending climax. After the war he had vowed never to take another man's life, but killing in the war seemed different because your enemy was unknown and just as likely a kindred individual as a scoundrel. But Garrett knew Decker and knew him to be a murdering scoundrel. Garrett anticipated the next day without worry. There would be

209

no remorse over his killing this man with those sinister scars on his cheek. Garrett relished the prospect so, he overstayed his allotted time for lunch. Realizing his mistake, he jumped up from the table, left some money on the counter and ran out the door and back to the store.

"What took you so long?" asked Peggy, as soon as he had returned.

So wrapped up in his own thoughts of revenge, Garrett had never considered whether or not he should tell Peggy what he had learned. He hesitated.

"I was just enjoying my meal so that I lost track of time," he lied.

"Now you don't expect me to believe that do you? I've eaten a meal or two of Maude's cooking and it's certainly not that good. You're hiding something."

"Maybe so, but there's not much to be said about it. I just ran into one of Decker's boys, that's all."

"Surely, you didn't get in another fight because you're not bloodied up."

"Thanks. That Murphy has really got you believing that all I do in a fight is bleed."

"Well, you have to admit you do get banged around pretty good. Now, what happened?"

"Ed Skinner was there all drunk and

mouthing off. He didn't know what he was saying, though, because he told me who killed your father."

"What?" she cried. "Who was it?"

"It was Decker, as you would expect. He thought your father was me."

"What do we do now?"

"Wait."

"Wait? For what?"

"Tomorrow. I told Skinner to find Decker and tell him to come to town then because I was going to kill him."

"Oh, no. I want him dead, but I don't want to risk you getting hurt too. I've already had enough losses these past two years."

"You sure don't put much faith in my ability to defend myself? I did pretty well against greater odds than this for four years."

"In a fair fight I wouldn't have as many fears, but few fights with Decker are fair. I doubt that you can get anyone but Billy to help you."

"I don't want him involved and I'm surprised you want your future husband to take up my fight."

"It's more than your fight; it's our fight because of Father's death. And quit talking about my future husband. Everyone seems

211

to think Billy is going to be my husband, but he hasn't exactly asked me yet."

"But I don't know that I would trust Billy. A man whose heart isn't in something does not make the best ally."

"Billy will be here tomorrow and he is going to help out. Whether you like it or not, he is the only ally you'll be able to find."

Garrett didn't answer. This was one instant he was not glad to see the decisiveness which had dominated Peggy's judgments since the death of her father. It was no use to argue with her because her mind was made up.

"You're sure stubborn, grown more so in the last few weeks. You've been seeing Murphy too much."

"Maybe I do see Billy most every night, but add it up and I'm around you more every day than him. Perhaps it's you that's been this bad influence."

"I'm just a hired hand."

"That's right," Peggy said with a wink, "but Father told me when he hired you he was hiring you for your gun, too. Maybe he could see something coming that I couldn't because tomorrow we're going to need that gun."

CHAPTER 9

Sunrise broke on Crossrock like a towering flame in the eastern sky. This day would be warm, clear and fresh. It was too beautiful a day to die because it hinted of spring and the rebirth of life, even in this desolate place. Spring was not far away and as Garrett awoke that fateful morning his thoughts were on how he would leave Crossrock when the weather warmed for good. Should he tell Peggy or just slip away into the night as quietly as he had ridden into Crossrock many weeks ago?

The beauty of the day stirred not his fears of dying, for Garrett had long ago learned the insignificance of life. Measured against the bloody panorama of the War Between the States, one solitary death, even if it were his own, would not weigh heavily in the saga that has eternally pitted man against himself, his fellow man and the elements for survival. Garrett had not lost his desire for survival, as he once thought he had when faced with the realities of his one-armed existence and the loss of his family, but that innate sense was overwhelmed by an inbred code of honor which required revenge for Dobbs.

The cowardly manner in which Dobbs was killed still plagued Garrett. Today, though, Garrett would settle the score and ease his conscience or die trying. He dressed slowly, putting on his gray pants and shirt, as a knight would put on his armor. For Garrett, this increasingly ragged outfit was his suit of armor — it had been with him in many encounters before. Next, he put on his worn but comfortable boots. That he had done without breaking his normal morning routine, but his next action bespoke the gravity of the day. He picked up his .44-caliber pistol and broke it down, dumping the cartridges from the cylinder onto the counter in the store front. He fetched a small can of gun oil from under the counter. Oiling the revolver, Garrett looked out into the deserted street. He was amazed by the beauty of the day. During his cavalry service, he had fought on much more scenic battlegrounds than the street through Crossrock, but he could not remember a day of battle more stunning and beautiful than this one was going to be. After a few well-placed drops of oil, Garrett gently pushed the empty cylinder back in place and spun it, listening with pleasure at the gentle clicking. He pulled the trigger a half-dozen times, getting the feel of his weapon back. Then, awkwardly, he reloaded the pistol with fresh ammunition from the stock in the store. Instead of reholstering it in his cavalry scabbard with the cover, Garrett took another holster from the case that held the ammunition. It was a newer, stiffer holster, but it would be better for fast retrieval than his worn army-issue holster. He backed against the doorjamb to put the gunbelt on in his awkward fashion. Then he pulled the gun out a couple times for the feel. It was not as bad as he had expected.

His main fear was generated by the trouble he had in loading his pistol with a single hand. That worried Garrett, who knew he would be at a disadvantage when it came to a gunfight, if he had to reload. Although he didn't like the idea of carrying the extra weight, Garrett took two of the pistols from under the gun counter for extra firepower. Loading them, Garrett left the pistols on the counter where he could pick them up quickly, if the need arose. When the confrontation did develop, as Garrett was sure it would, he would stick the two extra pistols in his belt. Finally, he took a handful of cartridges and stuck them in each of his pockets.

When he finished arming himself, Garrett realized how much earlier than normal he had arisen because Peggy still had not come to the store. She had not been late a single day since reopening the store for business after her father's death. He knew she would not be late today. Garrett took up a seat behind the far counter and sat silently watching the street and awaiting her arrival. Now there was nothing to do but wait. The next move was up to Decker and his friends. Garrett did not like being in a waiting position. He had learned in the cavalry that mobility and surprise were the best allies. Here he had neither, but then this was not a war like he had grown accustomed to. This was a dispute among men, not between nations, and the situation was unlike any Garrett had encountered before.

Garrett's father, though, had been involved in a duel once back in Alabama and had lived to tell about it. The elder Garrett's adversary was not that lucky. Although his father seldom talked about the killing, and then only reluctantly, Garrett remembered hearing that his father had not gotten off the first shot. Garrett recalled his father telling him that it did not matter who got off the first shot in a duel. What counted was who made the first hit. Perhaps that would be what was most important today. But would it be enough? In an even fight, perhaps so, thought Garrett, but he knew there would be no such certainty in fighting with Decker. The odds might be as great as five-to-one against him. Ever a realist, Garrett doubted that all of his first five shots would strike a target without his first being shot. Instead of spreading his shots around against other possible adversaries, Garrett knew that he would concentrate every shot on Decker until the ringleader was dead. After that, he would try for whoever appeared to be the greatest threat.

Garrett was still mulling over his strategy when Peggy walked past the window and unlocked the door. A few steps behind came Murphy, brooding at the prospect of seeing Garrett again.

"Morning," said Peggy, as she opened the door and stepped inside. "It's such a beautiful day for this time of year. Billy, now come on in here and quit lagging behind."

"It is a nice morning," replied Garrett, "and that makes it even nicer to see you out in your yellow blouse." Murphy stepped inside, grumbling to himself out of anger at Garrett's comment, which was much too intimate for his liking. Murphy, who put his shotgun down and closed the door, was further antagonized when Peggy walked over to Garrett and buttoned the sleeve on his good arm. That done, she held his hand for a silent moment, then spoke.

"Last night I found the envelope you gave me the night of my birthday. I had forgotten about it."

"So had I after what happened," said Garrett. The passages from Shakespeare now seemed meaningless in facing the day ahead.

"The tragic events of that night," continued Peggy, "seemed to make the passages more meaningful. I appreciate the hairbrush, but the envelope was much more special. Thank you."

Then, despite Murphy's presence, Peggy stepped up and pecked Garrett's cheek with another gentle kiss, like the one that had enraged Murphy the day of the funeral.

Peggy, though, seemed almost oblivious to Bill Murphy and never thought about the jealousy that burned within her companion. Like an enraged dog on a leash, Murphy was helpless to do anything. The veins in his neck stood out as he clinched his fist and reddened with anger at Garrett and the imposition that the Alabaman had made on his relationship with Peggy.

Looking up from Peggy, Garrett could see the rage in Murphy's face. For once, though, Garrett felt a tinge of sorrow for Murphy because he had seen in his eyes the hurt which was not completely hidden by his anger. That wounded pride and genuine remorse that Garrett had observed momentarily in Murphy's eyes left him thinking Peggy was only using him to hasten Murphy's marriage proposal. That kiss settled the question about Garrett's plans for the spring. Until then, the temptation to stay and vie with Murphy for Peggy's affections had been strong, almost overpowering. But Murphy's eyes silently spoke of his real love for the young woman, a love that Garrett knew would provide Peggy a home and security. Those were things which Garrett could not be assured of providing the brown-haired beauty. He had to prove too many things, like his ability to survive with a single good arm, without taking on the extra burden of a wife to support. It angered Garrett to think Peggy might be using him, otherwise why such an ostentatious show of kissing him in Murphy's presence. She seemed almost cold in her feelings.

219

"I wrote those lines a while back when I had thoughts of staying in Crossrock," Garrett said finally. "I am glad they had some meaning for you, but don't read anything into them on account of me because I will be leaving in two or three weeks."

"Who'll run the store with me?"

"You do a fair job yourself," said Garrett. "Anyway, I remember Murphy there telling you he could help out as much as needed."

"He only said it to get rid of you and he knows that."

"Maybe so, but don't you think he would help you out once I was gone?"

"What's gotten into you, Morgan? You know I'll need help."

"When I was hired, your father told me I was needed more for my gun than anything else. After today, there won't be a need for my gun. You know the store isn't doing that well right now, or you should. I sure do because I've kept the books. More people owe you than can pay and it's not going to change until some crops are harvested around here."

"But, you must stay," answered Peggy, whose eyes began to fill with tears.

Although he hated to see her cry, Garrett knew that the self-assured decisiveness which had been so characteristic of Peggy since her father's death was more of a stoic front than Peggy could maintain indefinitely. This was the good cry that Garrett knew she had not had since holding her dead father in her arms outside the store door.

Relieved that he had announced his intentions to move on, Garrett hardly believed how easy it had been to tell her. The one thing he had been dreading, that decision on whether or not to leave Crossrock and whether or not to let Peggy know, had been so easy after seeing Murphy's wounded expression. Garrett was uncertain why Murphy's feelings had affected him so because he still disliked the big man. But there was something intangible which bothered him, and his renunciation of Peggy and Crossrock seemed the thing to do, as if to assure that Peggy was not playing Garrett off against Murphy's emotions.

Murphy for his silent part in the drama was uncertain what to think. He, too, had a great dislike for the other man, so he was automatically suspicious. Still, there was something in the gesture by Garrett that Murphy realized was more than an admission of defeat in the battle for the love of Peggy.

When Peggy, bewildered over the sudden

change in Garrett and stunned by the thought of his departure from the store, began to sob, Murphy walked over and put his massive arms around her. He comforted her as best he could, while Garrett returned to his seat behind the back counter. The silence was broken only by the gentle sobs of Peggy. Garrett already had said what he felt had to be said and Murphy, still uneasy in Garrett's presence, let his caressing arms rather than his words try to soothe the feelings of the young blue-eyed woman.

At length Peggy regained her composure and went about her work in the store. No customers ventured to the store after opening time because most people had heard of Garrett's foolish challenge to Decker. Those folks preferred to be out of the way in case trouble broke out. As a result, only Peggy scurried about the store, doing the menial tasks which she always seemed to find.

Murphy, who had picked up his shotgun from near the door, seated himself by the front window in the chair that Peggy once spent so much time in reading her precious books.

For the uneasy trio, time passed slowly, as if it was inflicting an unbearable torture on the three who faced the uncertainty of the day. Garrett could tell that Peggy was nervous because she would start one chore before finishing another one. Then, she would remember what she had been doing only to drop the work on her next chore and return to her previous one. Garrett was unsure about Murphy, who was motionless except for his right foot which kept tapping the floor at intervals almost as precise as the ticking of a clock. As for himself, Garrett knew he was anxious for the showdown to come. His palm was sweaty, an indication of his subdued nervousness. The strangely slow and quiet morning passed without incident.

At noon Murphy took Peggy over to the Benton Saloon for lunch. After an uneventful thirty minutes, the two returned arm in arm. No words were exchanged by the three as Garrett got up from his seat, took one of the extra pistols from the counter and stuck it in his belt. Then he walked out the door and headed for lunch at the saloon.

Even Maude Benton was strangely quiet today, as though she were afraid to say anything. Garrett helped himself to the food that was on the counter and took a seat facing the door. He removed the pistol from his belt and placed it on the table. Cautiously, he began to eat his meal.

"I — ah — ah," Benton began nervously,

"I haven't seen a thing of Decker and his boys. How 'bout yourself?"

"Nothing."

"Sure makes me nervous. Think they're not coming?"

"They'll be here. Could be they're waiting for dark. They make braver night fighters."

"Uh-huh, it's a shame isn't it — those boys doing bad when there's so much to be done and so much gained in these parts now by an honest and strong young man."

Garrett didn't answer for he heard horses out in the street. His hand moved quickly to the pistol on the table and then retreated when he saw a team pulling a wagon past the saloon.

"What were you saying?"

"Doesn't really matter. I'm just trying to stay calm."

"He's been real nervous since yesterday. He's afraid Decker's coming here to harm him," said Maude Benton. "I've tried to keep him calm, but it's hard since he's scareder than I am."

Garrett knew that was a lie because Maude would be talking much more were she not terrified. Finally, realizing that part of her nervousness was over his presence and the fear that Decker would find him there, Garrett gobbled down his lunch.

Finished, he quickly got up, sticking the extra pistol back in his belt, and marched out the door.

"I'll see you two tomorrow when things should be settled down," said Garrett without looking back.

"I hope so, oh God, I hope to see you here tomorrow," said Maude Benton as the lame-armed man walked out and shut the door.

Back at the store, Garrett took the gun from his belt and placed it back on the counter. Then, he retreated to the same seat where he had sat quietly all morning.

After a strained silence, Murphy spoke up.

"Garrett, I make no bones about it, I haven't liked you since the moment I saw you outside of town. At first it was that coat of yours and then it was you borrowing Tom's watch from Peggy's father. Most of all, I resented the liberties you took with my Peggy and I still don't like that."

The Alabaman sat without moving a muscle, but with his eyes squarely on those of the red-haired, ruddy-faced Murphy. The big man paused for a moment, as if trying to decide what to say next. Garrett only waited, saying nothing, but noting that Peggy did not object when Murphy called her his girl. It was obvious from Peggy's silence that she was still angry at Garrett for his plans to leave. Maybe that affection which he thought had existed between himself and Peggy had only been his imagination and she had, in fact, been using him to speed up Murphy's matrimonial plans. It was too confusing to try to sort out now.

"But no matter," Murphy continued. "In spite of all of that Peggy and I owe a lot to you because you have been a help to us. No matter what has happened today or has happened in the past, you're welcome to stay."

"I'll be leaving in a couple weeks, no matter what. Let's just forget about the past, get done with today and then go our separate ways."

"You're welcome to stay here until you think it is time to be moving on. Peggy is grateful for the things you have done. I guess I am too, or at least for most of the things because you always came to my aid when I needed help. I intend to repay you today."

"You owe me nothing because most of what I did was for Dobbs, not you. I never came to your side that I didn't first weigh the risks to me."

"Still you came."

"Maybe so, but that doesn't mean you owe me a thing and it's probably best you stayed out of this fight because some people are going to die. I'd hate to see Peggy a widow before she even became a wife."

"I haven't sat here all day just to watch you fight them alone. There's a lot of work I could have gotten done at the place on a day such as this and I'm not going to waste it totally by not facing Decker, if he shows up."

"Suit yourself."

The conversation ended there. Peggy never said a word, just went about her business as if she were deaf to the talk.

By the middle of the afternoon, nerves had grown taut. Any noise from outside brought sudden glares from three pairs of eyes, all expecting the worst. But nothing had yet happened and Garrett began to wonder if perhaps his threats had scared away the adversaries he now longed to face. Such thoughts, though, were dangerous because they meant Garrett was underestimating the courage of his enemy. That could be a fatal mistake and Garrett knew it, but the tedium of waiting was beginning to take its toll on his nerves. But before those ideas could take hold of his mind and weaken his own resolve, Murphy spoke in an excited voice.

"Here they come — all five of them," he said, as he got up from his seat and pressed his face against the window.

Garrett, too, arose from his chair. He grabbed both spare pistols from the counter and thrust them into his belt. Stepping around the counter, he strode for the door, his heart pounding, pulse racing. Then he stood in silence watching the approach of the five horsemen.

Slowly the five riders drew closer. There was no jauntiness, no rowdiness, the usual signs of their visits to Crossrock, in their measured procession. Instead there was a seriousness, a deadly seriousness in their gait. Decker led. The other riders, four abreast, followed Decker's mount. As they passed the livery stable, Decker spurred his horse to pick up the pace. Riding by the store where Garrett, Murphy and the woman all stood at the window, Decker tipped his hat toward them in acknowledgement of their presence. Lucky Ed Skinner, whose drunken stupor had inadvertently tipped Garrett off to Dobbs's killer, spat as he passed. The man called Snuff never even glanced at the store, but kept his eyes on the leader. The two Norman brothers — Willie and Selmer — riding on the other side of Skinner and Snuff duplicated Decker's gesture in tipping their hats toward the store. Once past the store windows, Decker pulled his horse back into a slow walk and rode on to the Benton Saloon. Never did the five look back at the store, as if showing their disrespect for their opponents' fighting ability.

"Look at them," huffed Murphy, "riding into town like they owned the place."

"Maybe they do," Garrett answered. "They sure are cocky, but until now nobody's stood up to them."

"I'm not scared of them."

"Nobody says you are, but the fact is nobody has forced their hand until now. Just tell me who's the best with a gun?"

"Decker is supposed to be pretty good, but Willie Norman I have seen use a pistol and he's quick. I've heard Snuff is fast and the way he carries his gun, I suspect that's true. Selmer Norman is a poor shot. Ed Skinner is probably the worst shot, I think, because he is always either drunk or recovering from too much liquor."

"I want Decker. Who do you think you can handle?"

"It's not a matter of who I can, but who we should try for. Snuff's the one that's got me worried, so I'll try for him."

"After that, open up on whoever looks like the biggest threat."

"Fine, are you ready to go?" quizzed Mur-

229

phy, as he picked up his double-barreled shotgun.

"No, let's wait. Let's let them make the first move."

"You two be careful, please," begged Peggy in her first remarks in Garrett's presence since earlier in the morning when he told her he was leaving. "Is there any way out of this? There are five of them to you two. Maybe they'll go on through and not bother us anymore."

"Shut up, Peggy," said Murphy in the gruffest tone Garrett had ever heard him use on her. "This is our best chance to straighten things out here. Unless we fight now, there will only be me to face them when Garrett leaves. Eventually, somebody has to do it."

"But I'm scared now. I don't want to risk it."

"It's too late for that."

Garrett listened to them as he watched the Decker bunch dismount in front of Benton's saloon. The five went inside.

"They're over at the saloon," said Garrett, trying to get Murphy's attention back on the five men. "It's good, maybe they'll have a drink or two. That shouldn't hurt our chances any."

Minutes that seemed like hours struggled

by and still nothing. Then the saloon door opened slowly. It looked suspicious so Garrett pulled the pistol from his holster and Murphy raised his shotgun. Both put their weapons back when they saw Benton emerge from the saloon.

Benton walked deliberately, as if a gun were pointed at his back. From the instant he stepped outside the door and off the walk, it was evident he was headed for the store. The closer he got the more tentative his steps became. Garrett could see that Benton was not pleased with his mission nor secure about his safety.

Peggy opened the door for him as he neared the store. Inside he came, shaking visibly.

"They're there in my saloon with Maude," Benton stuttered. "They say they want you Garrett. Decker said for me to tell you he got the message and he's waiting to see if you can deliver it in person."

"You tell him I still intend to."

"Billy, Decker said to tell you he had no quarrel with you and for you to stay inside and you wouldn't get hurt."

"I don't intend on getting hurt inside or outside," said Murphy. "You tell Decker to step out of the saloon alone and I will stay out of the fight. But if he comes out with

231

any of his friends, I'll fight with Garrett. Can you remember that?"

"I guess so," said Benton, who was growing more nervous with each second he was in the store.

"Tell him to be outside in fifteen minutes," said Garrett, "and we'll settle up."

As Benton made the return trip to the saloon with his messages for Decker, both Garrett and Murphy began to check their guns a final time to be sure all was in readiness.

"Remember," said Garrett, "Decker is mine."

"I'll not argue with you because there'll be enough to go around."

Peggy was crying with tears streaming down her cheeks. Unlike the death of her father which had been so sudden and unexpected, this situation was more terrifying for it was building so slowly toward a conclusion that did not seem possible for both her men to come out unharmed.

She stood sobbing between Murphy and Garrett at the window, watching the saloon door. Then it opened and out stepped Decker, alone. Peggy's crying came to a halt as she held her breath, hoping nobody else would step out of the saloon and Billy would be spared the duty of following

Garrett to a brush with death. She knew that she had pressured Murphy into coming, although she was never sure he wouldn't have come anyway out of hate for Decker. Still, though, she regretted her part because it would weigh heavily on her mind if Murphy was hurt. An overwhelming sense of relief came over her as Decker moved toward the store alone. Billy would be spared, she realized.

But her relief was tempered by fear for Garrett now. Nothing could stop this drama. It was unlike the plots in her precious books — although the ending might not be a happy one — there was solace in that it was just a book, a story. This was no story. As Garrett straightened himself and reached for the door knob, Peggy grabbed him and hugged him with all her might. Garrett could feel her tear-stained cheeks against his. He was sorry for her and not bitter as he had been for awhile earlier in the day.

"It will be okay," he said. "It will be okay."

Out into the street he strode for a final showdown with the man that had been a source of ridicule to him from the first day he rode into town and had a meal at Benton's saloon.

Peggy and Murphy watched from the store as Garrett began to walk toward Decker.

But Garrett had taken no more than a half dozen steps out of the fifty that separated them when three more men emerged from the door of the saloon. It happened so unexpectedly that Peggy, who had been regaining her composure did not have a chance to grab Murphy and hug him before he had picked up his shotgun and run out into the street to walk with Garrett. Seeing that she had not even been able to kiss Murphy, Peggy now broke down under a flood of tears and self recriminations. Her worst fears were coming true. She sank from the window to the floor too scared to watch Garrett and Murphy. She did not want to risk seeing them die. She did not hear the yelling between the combatants because of her own sobs. As she cried, the two men in her life marched toward twice their number.

"Now, Billy," shouted Decker, "we've got no argument with you. It's just Lefty we want to even up with. All of us have something to settle with him."

"If you've all got to settle with him, then do it one at a time. If you decide to settle all at once with him, then you've got me to contend with too."

"Murphy," whispered Garrett, "where's Ed Skinner?"

"I don't know. Seeing as how he went into

a saloon, I bet he's had a drink too many to handle a gun."

"I still don't like it, though."

"Look, Garrett, we've got enough to handle with these four without worrying about Skinner."

"Remember, I've got Decker."

"I'll take Snuff. After that try to get Willie Norman because he's a better shot than Selmer."

When the two groups of men were about twenty paces from each other, both stopped. For a brief moment, they stood sizing one another up. Garrett stood to Murphy's left, wiggling his fingers to make sure there was no stiffness in them when it came time to make a play. Murphy stood with his shotgun cradled in his left arm, almost pointing directly at Garrett, and with his right hand on the triggers ready to swing into action, as if hunting quail.

Facing them were Decker on the extreme left, then Snuff, Willie Norman and Selmer Norman. Decker was grinning a sinister smile which accentuated those two thin scars up his right cheek. Snuff had spat a couple times as the two groups had moved closer. Willie Norman was expressionless and deadly threatening, but Selmer Norman seemed too nervous to be effective. Each of the four stood in a line with about four feet between them. Garrett and Murphy stood six feet apart.

Garrett broke the deadly silence.

"Tell me, Decker, with your own mouth that it was you that killed old man Dobbs."

"I regretted killing the old man," said Decker, "but I thought it was you, Lefty. Now, you answer my question. Skinner told me you said you was going to kill me. Is that true?"

"It is."

"Then here's your chance," shouted Decker, as he jerked his pistol from its holster.

Garrett drew, too, as he heard the report of Murphy's shotgun. Aiming his pistol, Garrett swung his right shoulder around to face the four and to cut down the size of the target that his body made. He heard Decker's shot whiz by, but without effect. He squeezed his trigger, thinking his bullet had hit its target, Decker's heart. But Decker still stood.

Murphy's shotgun blast sprayed buckshot into Snuff and Willie Norman, the middle two in the line of four. Although neither was down, both were injured. Throwing his shotgun down, Murphy had then drawn his pistol and fired again at Snuff, missing him.

Snuff and Willie Norman returned fire at Murphy, but inexplicably missed the behemoth of a target.

Garrett's luck was holding, too, because Decker's next two shots missed him. Garrett, following his father's advice, had not tried to fire all his shots as fast as he could. Instead, he fired a second one, more deliberately aimed than the first and Decker spun halfway around. Turning his attention to Willie Norman, Garrett blasted a bullet toward him and another toward Selmer Norman. The first hit its mark and Willie fell to the ground. Selmer, though, was still unscathed, but seeing his brother on the ground, he threw down his pistol and dropped to his knees over the dying Willie.

Four men were still standing, but only two were unharmed. And, those two had turned two-to-one odds into a decided advantage over their injured opponents. Firing the remaining shots in his pistol at Decker, Garrett grabbed one of the spare guns in his belt just as Decker fired another shot at him. Decker's aim was awry and Garrett had one more opportunity to down his opponent for good. This time his aim was deadly accurate and Decker fell back, flinging his gun over his shoulder in his death throes.

Although Snuff was still on his feet, he was having trouble standing and Murphy was about to finish him off when Garrett heard another shot that sounded as if it hit flesh. Garrett had lost his bearing in the fight, but he thought he had heard the shot come from behind him. Then when Snuff fell to the ground from another pistol shot of Murphy's, Garrett realized he must have been wrong. But no, another shot rang out and this time Garrett was sure it came from behind him.

"It's Skinner," shouted Benton, who had run out of his saloon. "In back of you in the livery stable."

"Come on, Murphy, let's go get the last one," shouted Garrett, who turned and fired at a crouching figure in the door of the livery stable.

Running down the street as fast as his suddenly queasy legs would move, Garrett tried to remember how many shots were left in his pistol. Four, he thought, but he couldn't be sure. Fortunately, he had the third pistol tucked in his belt.

Garrett looked over his shoulder at Murphy, who was following him, but at a pace that was little more than a walk. Reaching the stable door, Garrett flung it open to let as much light in as possible. In doing so, he saw Skinner in the loft overhead. He fired a shot and then dove behind one of the stable stalls just as a shot rang out. The shot missed, but in diving for cover, Garrett felt the extra pistol slip from his belt. Looking desperately, he could not find his extra weapon. Now he was down to two or three shots.

Glancing around the stall's edge, Garrett scanned the loft for Skinner. He did not see his assailant, but he did glimpse Holcomb, who lay on the ground, moaning and rubbing his hands over his bloodied head. Garrett was not certain whether Holcomb had been shot or just clubbed by Skinner. Garrett's eyes skirted around the darkened stable, looking for Skinner, but saw nothing. His ears, though, picked up an unnatural creaking in the loft behind him and he turned instantly to see Skinner taking aim at him. Firing as rapidly as his terrified fingers would allow, Garrett squeezed off two shots, the last of which knocked Skinner's gun from his hand and down onto the stable floor.

Garrett squeezed the trigger again, but the dull click told him and Skinner that he was out of ammunition. As he groped for the lost, but loaded pistol, Skinner jumped from the loft onto Garrett. The two desperate men rolled through the hay with each trying to gain a decisive hold.

When the two struggling men crashed into a stall wall, Garrett came up on top and pummeled Skinner with his good hand. But he was no match for the strong arms of Skinner, who grabbed Garrett's good arm with his hands and pulled the crippled man off.

As both got to their feet, Garrett took a swing which missed. Skinner, though, did not miss with his next punch and stung Garrett with a blow to the stomach. As Garrett doubled over in pain, Skinner knocked him to the ground with a ferocious punch to the nose and mouth. With Garrett downed and bloodied, Skinner jumped on him and grabbed the one-armed man around the neck. Garrett was in pain from the punches and now as Skinner applied the pressure to his neck, his struggle was nearing a fatal conclusion. As he grasped to break Skinner's grip, Garrett thought he saw Murphy standing over Skinner.

Although blood was in his eyes now, making it difficult and painful to see, Garrett was sure he had seen Murphy towering above him in his struggle with Skinner. But, if that was so, why had Murphy not come to his aid? His strength sapped, Garrett was losing consciousness for want of breath. Why was his ally not helping? Garrett's mind raged at Murphy, who was no better than Decker because he was going to stand there and let Skinner kill him. The peace that Garrett thought he had made with Murphy now seemed so hollow. Garrett only hoped he survived this beating because now he had one more score to settle.

Had it not been for Holcomb, Garrett would have had his life squeezed away by Ed Skinner. But the stableman, who had struggled to get up with his badly bruised head, grabbed a mallet when he saw Garrett's distress. Uncertain over Murphy's reluctance to give aid, Holcomb rushed up to the two men struggling on the floor and parted the hair on Skinner's head with a savage blow of the mallet.

"That's the one I owe you, Garrett, for saving me from Snuff," shouted Holcomb triumphantly.

But Garrett never heard him as he gasped for the breath that would help him recover his strength and unmuddle his mind. Holcomb tried to help him up after pulling the unconscious Skinner off him, but Garrett made no effort to arise. He stayed where he was on the stable floor, drawing in deep, replenishing breaths.

When the gunshots had ended, Peggy had picked herself up from the store floor, afraid to look out the window. Her first glance at the three bodies strewn on the dirt street had confirmed the reality of her fears, but as she moved from one body to the next she realized Garrett and Murphy were not among the dead. Running out the store door and following Benton's gestures toward the livery stable, she raced as hard as she could to see if everyone was okay. Once at the door of the stable, she had seen Murphy standing over a bloodied Garrett still lying on the ground. She screamed and ran to Garrett.

"How bad is it? Are you okay? What happened?"

Garrett did not even try to answer as Peggy attempted to stop the blood and clean up his bruised face. He was still catching his breath. When he could talk, Garrett was going to fire his words at Murphy for betraying their alliance.

With blood still dripping from his face, Garrett finally pushed Peggy aside and stood up, although somewhat wobbly for a moment. Then he spoke.

"Murphy, you son of a bitch, just going to let Skinner choke me to death were you? Let me get my gun because I've got one more difference of opinion to settle."

For a moment Murphy seemed to ignore Garrett's challenge. Slowly moving his glazed eyes, Murphy looked straight at Garrett.

"You never get in a fight without getting bloodied and bruised," said Murphy, who paused for a laboring moment before continuing. "Look at yourself. Another fight and you're as bloody as a carcass."

"I've got one more fight in me," Garrett retorted.

But Murphy didn't answer. His eyes slowly shut, his knees buckled and he crashed face down to the ground.

"Oh, my God," said Peggy, who leaped to his side. "He's been hit. In the back."

CHAPTER 10

For more than a week Peggy tended to Murphy and his wound in the bed that had been her father's before he died. It was a deceptive wound which did not look that dangerous for the first few days. But with no doctor near, just as there was no sheriff around to represent the law in the matter of the gunfight, the wound slowly turned ugly with the festering look of eventual death. Murphy realized its seriousness, not from seeing the wound, but from feeling the stinging annoyance turn into a burning pain that bloated his belly and made sleep impossible. Despite the pain, Murphy never allowed Peggy to hear a cry or a moan that would give away the true agony he was enduring.

But even the physical pain seemed insignificant compared to the mental anguish that Murphy was suffering. Here he was, a huge man of tremendous strength, who had fought through the war without as much as a scratch, and he was dying from the wound of a cowardly back shooter. A man who had fallen from the roof of the Dobbs store and then climbed back up as if he had slipped on a step, Murphy now faced the reality of death, something he had never given much thought to, even during the war, because he had always seemed to be invulnerable. The dreams Murphy had lived of turning his land into the most prosperous farm in West Texas and of helping Crossrock mature into a bustling city haunted him.

Then there was Peggy, whom he had longed to marry, but had put off until he was in better shape financially. That was the one regret which he could not shake. And now, that was the one dream which seemed the most important and the most out of reach. It was the one dream Murphy could have made a reality had he not been so obsessed with his other goals. It was this realization that he agonized most over.

After a week of conscious suffering, Murphy began to lapse into unconsciousness and fits of delirium. Peggy sat by during those delirious spells, holding his hand and answering the uncomprehensible questions that came to his tormented mind. Sometimes Murphy would yell, as if in battle, and at other times he would whisper, much as

Peggy remembered him doing during their courting days when they were alone.

"Why haven't you had Garrett come by?" he asked one day in a voice that rang of his former strength. "Won't he come?"

"I thought you were delirious and I never asked him," Peggy admitted.

"See that he comes by and that he not wait long about it, either. I must talk to him."

To fulfill Murphy's request, Peggy left him alone for the first time since he was wounded to go for Garrett, who had run the store by himself since the shootout. Her steps were swift for she did not want to leave Murphy alone long, yet her mind was tentative since she did not want to face Garrett. If he had never arrived in Crossrock or if her father had never hired him, as she had argued, perhaps the old man would still be alive and Murphy would not be dying. She knew he had kept the store going through these meager times, and she was indebted to him. Yet, those debts seemed meaningless to her now because the price had been paid not by him, but by her father and Murphy. Why did it take a tragedy for her to realize how much Murphy had really meant to her? Why had she ever thought she could love Garrett? Maybe he was more learned and

246

read more books than Murphy, but it had been weeks now since Peggy herself had read anything. With father's death, there was just too much work to be done and that had increased with Murphy's shooting. Now the books seemed so empty and meaningless compared to the real trials of life. Things were not as simple in real life as they were in her books, Peggy realized.

Even with that simmering hate that had built up toward Garrett, Peggy was shocked by the Alabaman's appearance. He had been in the back room when Peggy opened the door with a tinkling of the bells on the door knob.

"Be right with you," came Garrett's voice from the back.

Peggy merely stood in silence, waiting for him to come to the front. When he did, her mouth flew ajar. She had not been to the store since Murphy had been shot, using Maude Benton to run her errands. Now she stood in horror, looking at Garrett's still puffy and purple face. Around his neck was a dark bruise which gave a good account of the strength of Ed Skinner. Flustered at his battered appearance, she could only stand there forgetting what her mission was.

"How's Murphy?"

"I fear not well. His wound looks worse

with each day, but he's big and strong and surely will pull out of it."

"Hope you're right. Did you come for something I can get you?"

"You. Billy wants to see you. I must get back because he's alone, but you shut up the store as soon as you can and come on."

Peggy left and ran back to her house. Garrett was not five minutes behind her. He, like Peggy, had been shocked at the other's appearance. That beauty seemed strained now and her face haggard. Nursing Murphy with only slight relief from Maude Benton had taken its toll on Peggy Dobbs.

When Garrett was ushered into the bedroom by Peggy, he could tell by a glance that Murphy's time was not long. He had seen before the pallor, the one that had turned Murphy's ruddy face into a ghostly tintype, on the bodies of too many battlefield dead. Garrett's remorse for Murphy was genuine and he wished he could change places with him. Crossrock could use Murphy's two strong arms, whose contributions could never be matched by a one-armed man, even if he was intent on staying in town.

Murphy, whose eyes were shut and senses dulled by pain, stirred, as if some unseen voice had told him he had a visitor. Open-

248

ing his slowly focusing eyes, he looked at Garrett with almost the same glazed expression that Garrett remembered seeing when he struggled with Ed Skinner.

"Leave us and shut the door, Peggy," Murphy whispered.

Almost before she could get out the door and close it, Murphy addressed Garrett softly.

"You and I, Garrett, have had our differences, but I never betrayed you. I remember following you into the stable, but I don't recall anything once I got there. I went to help you, but I . . ."

Murphy's voice trailed off and his eyes shut.

"You never betrayed me. I know that, Murphy."

As if strengthened by the other's words, Murphy continued.

"Peggy told me I just stood there when Skinner was on you and after Holcomb knocked him off I just said something about how bad you were beaten. I don't remember it. I tried to help."

"You've got no apologies to make. Don't think you do. Now just try to get your rest so you can recover and get to work on that farm and house for you and Peggy."

"There'll be no house and no farm. I'll

249

not get up from this bed. You and I know that. Peggy may not. Help her understand. Take care of her for me will you?"

Before Garrett could answer, Murphy lapsed back into unconsciousness. It was an answer that Murphy would never hear, even if Garrett had answered.

Although Murphy lingered for two more days before dying, he was never again conscious. Peggy sat beside him the entire time, just hoping he would awaken for one last time and she could tell him she loved him.

CHAPTER 11

A final harbinger of spring, the morning that Murphy was buried offered the hope of new beginnings. It was a stunning morning without a cloud in the sky and with a limitless brown horizon greeting the deep blue heavens. The cooing of morning doves brought the perfect music to this land which could be so desolate and yet so stunning at the same time. It was a paradox of beauty and ugliness.

But the sparkling day did not dawn on the minds of those gathered at the Crossrock cemetery. Once more a funeral was in progress. There had been three burials more than a week before when Brad Decker, Snuff Garrett and Willie Norman were laid to rest. Then there had been no mourning, except by Norman's brother Selmer and possibly by Ed Skinner, both of whom had survived the battle with Garrett and Murphy. Selmer Norman, unscathed in the confrontation and "Lucky" Ed Skinner, miraculously still among the living, had not been seen since their kin and compadres were buried. And now, on this sterling day, the last victim of the shootout was to be buried, not fifteen paces from the resting site of his three enemies.

A special sadness permeated the air for Murphy was respected, though not necessarily liked, by all the folks of Crossrock. He provided Crossrock specially needed commodities — youth and honesty. Few such men had returned from the war and none that did displayed the drive that Murphy possessed. With his death Crossrock was almost a town of old men and young widows. When Dobbs had been buried, all the folks mourned, but the grief was tempered by the knowledge Dobbs had lived a full life. Such thoughts did not enter the minds of those at this graveside service, for Murphy's life had been cut short like the lives of many in his generation. All in the cemetery mourned, but Peggy grieved most. As a final scripture was read, she grabbed the arm of Maude Benton to steady herself. Maude, who had helped Peggy as the young woman stood constant watch over the dying Murphy, had almost become a surrogate mother. The solace that Peggy had found in

Murphy and Garrett after the death of her father now came from Maude Benton, who brooded over the young woman like a mother hen.

As he watched Peggy during the simple ceremony, Garrett was plagued by Murphy's request to care for the young woman. Only two weeks ago, Garrett would have welcomed such a request for there was still between him and the woman a spark of mutual affection. Now, though, Garrett could sense that Peggy resented him and his role in Murphy's death. Less than two weeks ago, only the living Murphy stood between Garrett and Murphy. Now following the shootout, the dead Murphy presented a more formidable barrier between himself and the woman. Garrett knew that wall existed because Peggy had hardly spoken to him since the day she came to the store to fetch him on Murphy's request. It was almost as bad as when Garrett was first hired over Peggy's objections and she had all but refused to admit his existence. Garrett's unbuttoned right sleeve was stark evidence that Peggy's attitude toward him had changed.

Garrett remained in the background as those at the funeral began to share final condolences, break up and go home. Peggy, sending Maude Benton away, tarried at the grave a few minutes longer before turning for her home. Garrett had been waiting for this moment. Softly he walked toward her, and as he did she looked up at him and their eyes met. Garrett did not see the coldness he had expected in her eyes. Instead it was more of a vulnerability overwhelmed by a pride which refused to acknowledge she might be wrong. Garrett searched his mind for the right words to speak, but nothing seemed appropriate. Instead it was Peggy who spoke first.

"Two years ago I would come out to this cemetery and look for wild flowers. It always seemed there were more here than anywhere else. I guess it was silly, but I always thought it was because the dead were trying to say a part of them is still alive. I know better now, but I doubt I shall ever pick flowers here again, not with Mother, Father and Billy buried here. There's a marker for brother Tom, but he was buried somewhere in Tennessee. All those that meant so much to me and now all that's left are three wooden markers and another on the way for Billy. It doesn't seem like it's really happening to me in a way. All of it so sudden."

"Life sometimes is unfair," Garrett answered with a pang of instant regret because it sounded so trite. "I mean death robs some of us more than others and you've been more unfortunate than most."

"Now I guess I know the pain you must have endured when you learned your wife and children had died. I remember when you first told me that, I felt sorry for you and yet secure in not losing more of my family. Now, I am just as alone as you."

"No more relatives?"

"Some of Mother's folks still live in Indiana, but it's been so long since we've heard from any of them that they may no longer claim me for kin. I'm not even sure they've found out about Mother's and Tom's deaths."

"Did Murphy have any family?"

"None that survived him other than an aunt who is still supposed to be back in Indiana."

"What are you going to do?"

"I don't know for sure. The Bentons have offered to take over the store and eventually buy me out, but I don't know. I may run it for awhile. If only Billy hadn't died. He was always so big and strong that I never figured he could be hurt, much less die. I guess that strength is what kept him alive as long as it did. Would you answer a question about Billy for me?"

"Sure."

"What was it that he wanted to see you for?"

"He told me that he hadn't betrayed me. He would have helped me out in the stable had he not blacked out."

"Anything else?"

"Most of all, he wanted me to agree to take care of you after he died."

"What did you tell him?"

"I never got a chance to answer because almost the instant he made the request he passed out."

"Then what would you have told him?"

"I can't say for sure. Probably would have depended on your feelings. I suspect, though, you blame me for his death and would just as soon me pass on."

Peggy paused, uncertain what to say.

"Maybe I do," she said finally, "but so much has happened in the last few weeks that I don't know what I think any more. I just need time to get straightened out."

"Perhaps you do need time, but spring is here and I will be moving on shortly. At most, that will be in a couple days."

"Won't you stay longer and help me with the store?"

"You know the store is barely hanging on now. You hardly bring in enough money to make it worthwhile for yourself, much less to support an extra hand."

"Things will get better, you just stay and you'll see."

"Don't fool yourself. There are no men in the fields. It's planting time and work should already have started for this year's crops, but there's no one to do the work. If there are no crops, there's no money to buy anything, but the necessities from your store."

"That's not true, better times are coming!"

"I'll ask you now to come with me in a few days. We'll get married and start afresh somewhere in the new country. I know I'm lame, but I'll support you as you would expect a two-armed man to do."

"But I can't leave here, not now. Maybe that's what you did in Alabama, but you were only running from your past."

"Running from my past?" Garrett's voice rose. "I'm not running because your past is something you can never escape. I'm just seeking a new beginning, a fresh start. That's what you need, too."

"What I need is some time, I've told you. I can't make a decision on marriage on the same day Billy is buried. Can't you see that?"

It was useless to argue with her, Garrett could tell. He wondered whether she would have accepted his proposal had it been offered before Murphy was shot. For that, though, there was no answer, or, if there was, it existed only in the mind of a God who had wrought too much sorrow in too short a time on both Garrett and Peggy.

As Garrett walked Peggy back to her house, he put his good arm around her and drew her body close to his. He knew it was the last time he would see her. Tomorrow morning early he would leave Crossrock. The fine weather would hold and staying in Crossrock would only serve as a daily reminder to Peggy of the tragedies that had befallen her loved ones during his stay. Although he was disappointed to have to leave her behind, he could only deal with her refusal to marry him by moving on. Even if he stayed the extra time she desired, the result might still be the same and he did not want to leave embittered. If he left now, the hurt would not turn to bitterness.

When the couple reached Peggy's front door, Garrett turned her toward him and kissed her on the forehead. She did not resist the kiss, but neither did she encourage it. Instead, when Garrett's lips lifted from her flesh, she turned toward the door and let herself inside. As she closed the door gently in Garrett's face, she barely whispered, "I'll see you in the morning."

Garrett, realizing that would not be, only said, "I hope you get to feeling better."

With that the door shut, as if the final page of one of Peggy's books had been turned and another story finished.

Before going back to the store, Garrett walked to the livery stable. Finding Holcomb, Garrett told him to have the horse ready for riding before dawn in the morning. Then he settled up with Holcomb, who refused to take but a fraction of the cost of caring for the chestnut because Garrett had helped rid the town of the hated Decker.

Finishing his business with Holcomb and confirming once again that his horse would be ready by dawn, Garrett began his final journey to the Dobbs General Store. Once there in what had been his home for the past fourteen weeks, Garrett began to collect his meager belongings. With some of the money that Holcomb had refused, Garrett picked out a change of clothes, some cartridges for his pistol, a blanket for his bed and some food for his meals. He left more than enough money on the back counter to cover the purchases. Even so, he still had about two dollars left. Realizing

Peggy would probably need the money more, he added another dollar to the total. Then he wrote a note explaining the purchases.

Garrett went into the back room and sat down on his cot, waiting for darkness. His mind was empty, as if drained by the events of the past two weeks, and he just looked around the room aimlessly. There was the desk where he had kept the ledger for the store. Beside the desk was the bookshelf with part of Peggy's library. Around the room his eyes jumped to take the clutter in one last time because Garrett wanted to leave early in the morning to avoid encountering Peggy, if she should come in before her normal arrival time. As his eyes ranged across the room, they kept coming unconsciously back to a dress box that he had noticed once before. After this had happened a dozen times, Garrett realized it was the gift that Dobbs had gone back to the store to get the night he was shot. Peggy had not found it? He got up from his cot and went to fetch the box. Sure enough, the ribbon was unbroken and he could tell something was still inside. In the morning he would leave the box and a note of explanation on his cot. Garrett was tempted, just like the first time he found the box, to open it, but he refrained again out of respect for Dobbs. As darkness buried the day, Garrett put his meager belongings and supplies on the desk and draped his long, gray greatcoat over the desk chair. Then he went to bed his last night in Crossrock.

Peggy was indeed early the next morning, but she was too late to catch Garrett at the store. When she opened up she had not seen the key that Garrett had slipped under the door after locking up an hour earlier. The store was too quiet, she observed. She only surmised it was one of the rare times when Garrett had overslept. For some reason she was anxious to see him. Maybe she could love him after all and maybe it wouldn't take her as long to decide as she had thought only hours ago.

When she spied the money and the note on the counter, she rushed into the back room and gasped when she saw the cot, empty except for a dress box. Running to the front door, she charged out into the still empty street and looked to the west. Only the vast emptiness met her eyes. Back into the store she raced, as if to confirm that what she feared had actually happened. Indeed it had, for Garrett's bed was empty except for the dress box.

On top of the box was another note in

Garrett's handwriting. It read:

This must have been what your father came for the night he was shot. I found it earlier, but didn't think it the right time to show you. Sorry I forgot until now.

Peggy was crying, but she was unsure whether it was because she held in her hands the last gift from her father or because Garrett had left.

Slowly, with an uncertainty of what to expect, she lifted the lid from the box. Inside was a wedding dress, her mother's wedding dress, the dress her mother had promised her when Peggy was just a girl. She pulled it from the box and held it in front of her. She knew it would fit, but although the dress promised of the future, it could not bring Garrett back.

ABOUT THE AUTHOR

Preston Lewis is the Spur Award-winning author of more than 30 western, juvenile and historical novels on the Old West as well as numerous articles, short stories and book reviews on the American frontier.

Lewis wrote the well-received "Memoirs of H.H. Lomax," a comic western series published by Wild Horse Press. "Bluster's Last Stand," the fourth book in the series, was published in 2017. Previous books in the series in order of publication were "The Demise of Billy the Kid," "The Redemption of Jesse James" and "Mix-Up at the O.K. Corral." The latter two were both Spur Finalists from Western Writers of America.

His western "Blood of Texas," originally written under his Will Camp pseudonym, received WWA's Spur Award for best western novel. Lewis's 2016 western "The Fleecing of Fort Griffin," another comic novel, received the Elmer Kelton Award for best creative work on West Texas from the West Texas Historical Association. It was Lewis's third Kelton award.

Lewis's True West article on the battle of Yellowhouse Canyon also won a Spur Award. His book publishers have included Bantam, HarperCollins, Pinnacle and Eakin Press. His short works have appeared in publications as varied as Louis L'Amour Western Magazine and Dallas Morning News.

Eakin Press published his three young adult novels on animals from frontier Texas: "They Call Me Old Blue," "Blanca is My Name" and "Just Call Me Uncle Sam."

When he is not writing or researching, Lewis enjoys traveling and photographing historic sites of the Old West and the Civil War.

The employees of Thorndike Press hope you have enjoyed this Large Print book. All our Thorndike, Wheeler, and Kennebec Large Print titles are designed for easy reading, and all our books are made to last. Other Thorndike Press Large Print books are available at your library, through selected bookstores, or directly from us.

For information about titles, please call:
(800) 223-1244

or visit our website at:
gale.com/thorndike

To share your comments, please write:
Publisher
Thorndike Press
10 Water St., Suite 310
Waterville, ME 04901